ALINGUARD

ALEXZANDER CHRISTION

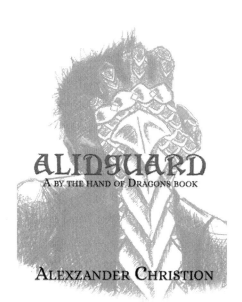

ALINGUARD

A BY THE HAND OF DRAGONS BOOK

ALEXZANDER CHRISTION

AlinGuard

By the Hand of Dragons

Copyright © 2018 Alexzander Christion

All rights reserved.

www.bythehandofdragons.com

Cover image by Johanne Light

http://johannelight.wixsite.com/portfolio

Edited by Off the Shelf Editing

https://www.facebook.com/offtheshelfediting/

Cover and book design by The Dust Jacket Designs

https://thedustjacketdesigns.weebly.com/

For permission requests, write to the publisher, addressed:

"Attention: Permissions Coordinator"

Ambition Publishing

1412 Taney Ave

Frederick, Maryland 21702

❀ Created with Vellum

DEDICATION

I dedicate this book to Herb Green, who told me if you shop in the garbage, the best you'll ever get is trash. Reach for the stars, you just might get an angel. Herb was right.

THE STORY THUS FAR

This story takes place between Books Three and Four.

Shefa was created by powerful dragon magic to be the perfect soldier. He was trained in Fuumashon, a land hidden away from the world for five-hundred years. While the rest of the world evolved technologically, Fuumashon evolved mystically. After the war Shefa was created to win was over, the magic that hid Fuumashon away was destroyed. Now he finds himself in a world more sky-ships and machines than scrolls and mages.

Magic still exists in the "Wider World," but it has been modified into a power source. Instead of burning wood or coal, most countries have power grids, weapons, vehicles, and defense systems powered by various forms of Arcanum. Any use of magic not approved by THE SINGULARITY is strictly forbidden.

The globe-spanning government, run by an elected Lord Regent who is little different than a king, controls every aspect of life on Earth. Shefa, having served his purpose of creation, defeating a foe capable of subjugating the entire world, has decided to spend his new-found freedom exploring the world he didn't know existed.

This is his first adventure.

WHITE AND BROWN

*"I picked a direction and started walking; were I wise, I would have brought
a map."*

The wind was never a thing to fear in the south. This far north, the wind could flay a man alive. It cut through cloth and flesh with equal ease, penetrating down to the bone. And the howling! The wind wailed with a panicked urgency, a neglected child in a small room. However, he was a king now; complaining was beneath him. But damn, it was cold.

Shefa decided asking; he should know his kingdom, tit andtittle. He could've had Raymond or Patience whisk him to the top of the world with a spell or a portal, but he chose to walk. Three days by foot, one week by horse, three months by ship until the ocean itself froze.

Ninety-two days of walking had hardened the few soft parts remaining, leaving him as cuddly as a plank of wood. Fitting for his current disposition. Between mountains of stone and snow, he spotted a thin line of smoke crawling up the overcast sky. Smoke meant fire, which meant civilization, people, and most importantly, warmth.

The small town was a series of wooden buildings, all similar sizes and shapes, organized in loose rows and columns. This was no town of inbred barbarians; someone here was learned. Shefa approached the nearest building, the one whose chimney promised thawed toes, and pushed inside.

The building was wood-faced; it looked like a modern cabin of sorts from the outside, but inside was red brick like the walls of a castle. The large room had only seven people in it. Five men. They wore no furs which surprised him since the snow was knee-deep outside, but when you live in *this,* you grow accustomed. None of the men were large, another shock, but they were just as ugly as he expected from a place so secluded. They looked at him with a mixture of fear and fury. He was too cold to care why.

"Greetings, stranger. Long way from home. What would the Kalmar have of us today?" a sweet yet manly voice said from the nearest table. Brown hair, brown eyes, brown clothes. Shefa decided to call him "Brown."

"I've never been this far north. Where am I?"

"This is AlinTown. Wait ... you marched across the White Death without supplies and you didn't even know where you were going? Are you mad?" Brown asked respectfully.

"Yes."

Shefa looked around at the plain, pale faces staring up at him from their simple tables and simple lives, trying to find something interesting to use as fuel to pretend he was good at conversation. Shefa was used to being stared at, especially up close. He stood six feet tall, thin but broad-shouldered and muscular. He'd spent his childhood in a mine and his twenties at war. He was built to give and take punishment.

A chatter went through his teeth and spine and he abandoned courtesy. The fireplace! He searched the room but didn't find one. He peeled off his gloves and dropped them where he stood. His fingers barely responded to his commands. The room was warm, almost uncomfortably warm ... how, no fire? His coat slid off his shoulders and hit the ground, more like ice than fabric.

"Sure. Put that where ever you please," Brown said with trained acceptance.

Shefa looked at the mess he was making, for the first time realizing that here he wasn't a king, just some ass making a mess before even introducing himself.

"My apologies. I am Shefa, king of all Fuumashon, firstborn to the emerald mistress Emmafuumindall, future king of all the world." He bowed.

Brown searched his friends for recognition. Heads shook and shoulders shrugged in response. "The Kalmar didn't send you, did he?"

"No," Shefa said simply.

"Well then, Shefa, I am Kayton, baker of bread, server of drinks, son of Dalton, and future lord of this fine establishment."

"This place has a name?"

"The ... Food Hut, my liege. Or ... grace. Lord?"

The mockery was clear this time.

"Shefa is fine. Where I'm from, titles only tell strangers who to ask about what. Kings die just like bread bakers. I know; I've killed them both."

The room blanched. Maybe casually mentioning murder was commonplace back home, but apparently it was frowned upon in the tundras. It was then that Brown noticed the things that always made people remember Shefa's face, like the rich brown skin and a strip of snow-white hair growing from his widow's peak amidst a dark brown mane.

And of course, his eyes. They were just a hair too wide, too wild, and his irises were like looking at stained glass windows. Shards, splinters, and slivers of blue, orange, red, brown and green were cut together seamlessly like the work of a master artisan. No one *ever* forgot those eyes.

"So, what brings you out to the middle of nowhere, sir, umm, King?"

"Shefa. I grew up in a cave in the south of Fuumashon. If I'm gonna be king of the world, I figure I should see my kingdom. Get to know my subjects. Help them where I can. That's the whole point of being king."

Shefa forced a friendly smile. It didn't go over well.

The men in the room looked at each other then burst into laughter. Shefa looked around, confused. He might have taken offense but he was too cold to be offended. He flexed his fingers. They responded. They hurt.

"I missed the joke."

"If you think the job of the king is to make life better for the little folk, you're not like any king I've ever heard of."

Kayton wore a very particular smile, the kind a man wore when his cards were better than yours and he knew it.

"I haven't met any human kings yet. At least not any I didn't crown myself."

Well, one, Shefa thought as he took a seat and pried his boot off. His toes were a sick color and the skin looked like burned bark. The nails came off with the shoe.

"So not just a king, but a kingmaker, as well?" Kayton spun back to the room, making a show of how funny he found this stranger. "You're very accomplished, aren't ya? Not even twenty summers under ya belt and you're being king, making kings, marching to the ass-end of icebergs ... and all for the good of the people."

The room tittered with laughter while Shefa struggled to get his toes to respond to his commands. He looked around. They were mocking him, but he didn't know how ... or why.

"Kayton?"

"Your high and mightiness," he answered with a dramatic bow.

"Get me something not very precious to you. This will all go smoother once you know who I am. Anything you can live without will do."

Kayton looked around to his friends; even the women were involved now. He shrugged and grabbed a plain wooden cup from behind the bar.

"Will this work?" Kayton asked, on the verge of snickering.

"Splendidly. I'm told that magic is forbidden in the wider world. I assume this place is warded," Shefa said. Kayton looked confused. "Wards. Spells of binding that prevent the use of magic," Shefa explained.

"I know what wards are, stranger. 'Course the place is warded; that's why the fire in the walls don't burn the place down," he said with a shake of his head as though it were common knowledge. And who knows? Around here it probably was.

"Ah. I wondered about the heat. No fireplace." Shefa flashed a childish grin at his own cleverness. It didn't help his standing in the room.

"What do you plan to do, mister?"

"No worries, Kayton, baker of bread, server of drinks, son of Dalton, future owner of the Food Hut. No harm will come to any but this cup."

Shefa sat the cup on the table, flexed his stiff fingers, and focused. The cup levitated up from the table, hovering a foot above his head where everyone could see it, whirling silently in space. Shefa had their attention. He banged a hand on the table, startling them all; at the same time, the cup split into eight perfectly equal pieces. Each piece hovered, twirling like circling birds.

He looked around. They weren't impressed; they were scared. No magic should work in here but there he was, magicking!

"How?" Kayton got out with just enough *oomph* to produce sound.

"I am a Psion. Some call it 'Mind Magic.' This is a parlor trick. I once did this to a man. It wasn't nearly as neat."

No sound existed in that room. The pieces floated across the space above the tables, one to each of the patrons, and dropped on the table with a startling clickity-clack. One woman went to pick up the piece in front of her and her male companion smacked her hand.

He looked at Shefa, Shefa looked at him. A small nod of trust passed between them and the man plucked the piece from the table. The other patrons followed his lead. They seemed marveled at the finger-wide slice of wood in their hands. Shefa smirked despite himself.

"Magic is outlawed around here; you're gonna end up in a cell, mister!" Kayton managed.

"I know nothing of this land or its laws, but worry not. Such stupid things will soon be stricken down. Progress is not to be doled out by fat men in rigid chairs, and I will have none of it in my kingdom."

A voice of dissension in the back burst to life. "Get out! Get out and don't come back! He's gonna bring the Kalmar's men down on us with this."

"Oh, really? Ya think so? Figure one of them is hiding out in the snow, watching in case a stranger shows up? Sit down, Dale. You're dumber than you are stupid. Coward."

Kayton seemed disgusted to have spoken to the man. Shefa didn't like Dale. He wondered how long before a reason to kill the man would present itself.

"Shefa, mister king, sir. That's a neat trick and all, but what exactly is this supposed to prove?"

"Take a piece."

"What?"

"The cup; take a piece."

Kayton looked around again. The men shook their heads, but the women egged him on. He grabbed a plank of the cup and held it between index and thumb.

Shefa spoke into his mind. *"If you drop the wood, you will look weak for the rest of your days."*

Kayton's eyes widened at the intrusion but he held on to the wood.

"Ready?"

Kayton nodded.

Shefa threw a flip of the hand and the wood burst into green flames. Kayton yelped. The women squealed. The men slid back in their chairs with a squeak only wood on wood can make. Kayton held on. The flames didn't burn. It was a trick, an illusion. He smiled at the prank, thinking himself clever until the smoke hit him.

The wood burned savagely. He watched it blacken and shrivel between his fingers, dying in his hands from a flame that didn't seem to notice his presence. The room looked on in open-mouthed fascination as wood became ember and smoke. Even the ash burned down to nothing.

"Do you have any idea how much control it takes to burn a thing and NOT burn the man holding it?"

No one moved. No one spoke. One woman blinked.

"I am Shefa, king of Fuumashon. Firstborn of the emerald mistress, Emmafuumindall. Future king of all the world. How good is the bread?"

Shefa spent the next three days meeting the folks of AlinTown, all forty-seven of them. He visited every building, all seventeen. AlinTown was a refugee haven. Bigger towns like AlinHold, the fortress; Alin-Height, high in the mountains; and the capitol, AlinHall, were constantly under siege these days and those with nothing keeping them rooted to the city moved out here. Peace over prosperity.

The town crier, Holter, wanted nothing to do with the strange man and was happy he had chosen Kayton as his guide. Shefa was given furs and snow boots to replace the gear he'd left home with. He was almost finally warm from his march.

The most important thing he'd learned in his three days with Kayton was a small problem the region was having with bandits. According to Kayton, who he still called "Brown," AlinGuard, the most secure prison in the world, had been taken over by the inmates and now served as their base of operations. Shefa thought they would ask him to do something about the snow, or food, or women, but no; they just wanted the bandits dead so they could go back to their shitty existence of sucking life from snow.

Shefa had been given a small room in the "crooked" building. It had an official name, but he couldn't be bothered to learn it. Most buildings faced south away from the howling wind, but this building faced south-west for some reason. No one could tell him why. In fact, until he mentioned it, no one even seemed to notice.

Kayton joined him in the small room. Shefa liked it because it was small enough to keep warm, even at night when the cold became a living thing, vicious and eager for toes.

"Tell me, why hasn't the king handled these bandits?"

"No king wants to lose. Makes him look bad."

Shefa was puzzled. "A king cannot control bandits in his own kingdom?" he asked incredulously as if he had just been told that the sun was a ball of gas burning millions of miles away in frozen space.

"Not for lack of trying. Soldiers, knights, and sellswords all marched out to the north; what few came back were broken in body and mind. Evil lives in those peaks, and not just the men."

Now he was intrigued. These bandits were starting to sound like worthy adversaries.

"Start at the beginning. Tell me a tale," Shefa said.

Kayton lit up. He rubbed his hands together and put on a show.

"Legend has it that the prison known as AlinGuard was constructed by dwarves a thousand years ago, back when this land was warm. When the snows came and didn't leave, they moved underground, abandoning the castle for good. The nomadic tribes made a home of it. For thirty generations, it was the center of everything west of BerkenSpire.

"When prince Gaag came of age, he didn't want his father's throne and set out to build his own kingdom. He crossed the Polyphyodont Mountains and found a patch of earth the snow never seemed to find. He built a fort there. Tamed the land. Drove off the Cetacea and ruled in peace for twenty years."

Shefa appeared to be daydreaming, captured by some far away thought that made his eyes unfocused and his breathing stop. Kayton watched to see if he would return. Shefa didn't appear to come out of his trance but he spoke.

"There is a place in these gods-forsaken hills not covered with ice and snow and you live *here*?"

"Shall I continue?"

Shefa nodded smartly without ever breaking his faraway gaze.

"When the residents of AlinGuard learned of the paradise over the mountains, they fled in droves and begged for parlay. As his father's people, he accepted them into his kingdom. AlinHall became the new capital and AlinGuard became a prison. It was easy to run; very few guards needed since escape meant death. Nothing lived there; nothing grew there without assistance from the hall. A prison sentence was a death sentence."

"How did they get supplies?"

"The penal system in AlinHall was simple yet effective. Small crimes got you sentenced to work the fields. That's how enough food was produced to feed the inmates. Larger offenses got you sentenced to transport supplies to the prison. And of course, capital offenses got you sentenced to that frozen asshole. Many have attempted escape. The ones that made it outside were simply watched as they fled in vain only to freeze to death before they got anywhere near civilization."

"Brutal yet effective. I like this king."

"I'm sure you do."

"So, when did it all go wrong?"

Kayton thought for a minute and looked genuinely perplexed. "Nobody really knows. I guess a team went out and didn't come back. That's the only thing I can figure would start the questions. But the real question is: after they overpowered the guards who were probably overconfident in their safety measures, after they took the prison, how did they survive? Nothing goes out there. Nothing lives out there, yet somehow they not only survived but thrived."

Shefa was mulling it over it. The answer was obvious, but that didn't make it any simpler. They clearly had outside help, someone on the transport team most likely. This person might have already been an agent of someone inside who'd got himself sentenced to that particular detail in order to facilitate the escape. But why? Loyalty? Money? Power? Shefa packed it away for later.

"Continue."

"Not much more to tell. Everyone kinda figured they'd all die up there and the problem would sort itself out."

"That obviously didn't happen, so what did happen?"

"I don't know. Years went by, decades. Not a peep. The place was rumored to be haunted even before this, so nobody wanted to go there now. Crime just stopped. The threat of that place was more than enough. Then one day, bandits struck. They hit AlinTown, a small hamlet outside the capital. Nobody knew where they'd come from. The king's men scoured the land but came up empty. Then it happened again and again. Finally, men were stationed in all the hamlets and townships. When the bandits struck, they killed a good many of the king's men, trained soldiers, all of them!"

"If all the king's men died, how did you find out who was responsible?"

"I didn't say 'all,' did I? Scouts rode out after them. Followed them all the way to the Wicked Pass—that's how they figured out at least some of the prisoners had survived," Kayton answered, scratching his chin and looking far away as if a horrible memory were trying to crawl out of the back of his mind.

"Is this when the king sent his men?"

"Well, there was a little more that happened, but essentially yes. He sent a battalion. One hundred and fifty men, thirty cavalry. They took the pass and stormed the prison, armed to the teeth. Maybe it was the Nil stones. The prison is filled with them; can't have convicts using magic, now can ya? Maybe it was the long ride or the bitter cold." Kayton shrugged, a helpless thing, then brushed a non-existent hair from his face.

"Finally, what is it about these bandits that makes them so difficult to deal with?" Shefa asked at last.

Kayton seemed perplexed by the question. "Are you serious? You're serious, aren't you?" he asked.

Shefa didn't move for many seconds. He noticed Kayton didn't even blink. The man sighed like he had suddenly taken on a great load.

"They were prisoners," Kayton said.

"Yes."

"Prisoners."

"You said."

"At AlinGuard!"

Kayton waited for epiphany to strike, for the obviousness of the situation to dawn on the stoic stranger, but several heartbeats passed without any sign of blooming insight.

"What do you know about AlinGuard? Have you heard *no* rumors about it?"

Shefa shook his head. "None."

Kayton made a gesture that held no meaning to Shefa.

"AlinGuard is a prison, a *super* prison. It's not some construct of steel and stone to house rapists and murderers; we got a hundred of those in the Whitelands. AlinGuard is for the worst of the worst. It's not where you put men; it's where you put monsters."

Shefa, despite himself, smiled; a slow creeping thing of curious malice. "Tell me more about these monsters."

"Just so you have some idea what you're up against, Ballen, probably the most famous but likely not the most dangerous prisoner ever sent there, was convicted of attempted divinicide, the murder of the god Xalis, master of wind and war. Like I said, these are not men; these are monsters."

The warning played again and again in Shefa's mind as he ate ferociously. He consumed a meal of bread and meat fit to power a marching army.

He had decided to go see the king. He'd had his fill of trudging through knee-deep snow a week hence; so this time with a guide and a clear heading, he would travel more conveniently to the capital. With a small bag packed and strapped to his back, he found in a clearing far enough from any building; hopefully, to not level them with his exit.

"Last thing you need to know if you're really gonna do this..."

Shefa turned his head to the man but said nothing.

"The king is Kalmar; I use the word 'king' to not confuse you."

"Fail," Shefa said simply.

Kayton threw a snarky face back. "Kalmar Grond is a warrior. He respects strength. He won't abide disrespect of any kind. His guards are chosen for their brutality. He will make you wait weeks if it suits him, his way of seeing how desperately you need him."

"I'll wait one hour."

Kayton shook his head. "They only way you'll see him that fast is if you are announced as a monarch, which you won't be because no one in the north has ever heard of you."

Shefa nodded, a smirk tugging the corner of his lips.

"It was a pleasure to meet you, Shefa, king of Fuumashon, future king of all the world. May your death be swift and painless," Kayton said with a slow nod, squinting against the freezing, stinging wind.

"It was a pleasure to meet you Kayton, son of Dalton, friend of the throne of Fuumashon, future owner of a fine establishment. May your death be swift and painless," Shefa said with the same long nod.

Kayton looked at him curiously. "You know that's no common saying, right? Around here, we just say farewell."

"So why did you say it to me?"

Kayton barked out a laugh. "Because this is the last time I'm going to see you. You'll be murdered to death by morning!" He finished with another bark of rolling laughter.

Shefa held out his hand and closed his eyes. Emerald light flashed in his palm and Azreal's staff appeared, a three-quarter staff made from a branch of the great white tree that grows at the bottom of the world. It glittered like crystal in the muted grey sunlight. The bone-white staff was covered in one hundred layers of diamond dust, polished smooth as a mirror's surface.

"Hold this. I'll collect it on my return," Shefa said with a wink.

Kayton, open-mouthed, took the staff and nodded smartly as he accepted the priceless gift.

"Now back away. Less than fifty paces and you'll regret it."

Kayton didn't question, just started counting his steps as he backed away.

Shefa fell away. His mind left his body, going to that hall between realms where energy exists without matter, where the stuff of magic is summoned and shaped to change reality on the material plane. He found the stream of energy that spun the world: raw untampered velocity, enough to roll the whole world over and over for a billion years.

He siphoned off a sliver, the tiniest thread he could grasp, and sipped from the ancient fountain. Power poured into his body, filling it. His bones ached. He could feel his heart punching his chest from within. He teeth vibrated in his skull, sending a pain he had no name for up and down his spine before radiating out of his forehead.

Shefa opened his eyes; thick green energy billowed like smoke from glowing sockets that saw more than any eyes could. Light, life, the ebb and flow of air; he could see them all. He could see space, time, and the pulsing light of souls. He was no longer a creature of the material plane. He existed where the gods roamed and he had none of their divinity.

Shefa released a modicum of the kinetic energy at his disposal and tore from the earth in a storm. The barrage of thunder echoed off the mountains thirty miles away. Thousands of years of snow and ice sublimated, going from stone-hard ice to invisible steam without ever becoming water. Buildings bowed away from the blast, screaming as they fought to maintain structural integrity. Shefa was on the ground one second, a mile in the sky the next.

Kayton was blown off his feet. He rolled and bounced through a world of fog too thick to let him fall and slammed into something hard enough to stop him. A moment later, a violent gale blew it all away, leaving him panting, pinned against the food shack. He looked to the sky, to the emerald pulsing beacon hovering there, and for a moment wondered if this strange king from the south could do what he believed he could.

With a *boom* that blew a hole in the ever-present clouds, Shefa shot across the sky. A green star cut a line across the heavens until he disappeared from sight. Kayton watched for a few seconds more, and then remembered he held a Kalmar's ransom in his hands. His smile near swallowed his ears. He figured he should wait at least a week to be sure the fool was good and dead before he broke it into pieces and built a fort to make his ancestors proud.

"Now ... where to hide you?"

2

A MEETINGOF CONS

"You don't have to respect me as a person, but you will respect me as a threat."

Shefa knew his directions were true when a rolling patch of green crawled over the horizon, the only color in an infinite limbo of white. The ring of mountains surrounding this place kept the weather out, but let the water and livestock in. It was a hidden paradise. How they'd ever found it, he couldn't say.

He landed like a new bird: half stone, half tumbleweed. Flying was still a new trick in his bag. He took a moment to enjoy standing on earth instead of ice. It was a strange feeling, grass under his boots again. The feel of his weight pressing into the soil was oddly comforting.

It's amazing what you can come to miss, he thought to himself.

AlinHall was impressive. It was a castle fifteen levels tall, walls made of red stone which gave them a haunting glow in the meager sunlight. In the south, buildings were wide and squat, designed to help them shed the brutal heat, but in a frozen stain of a city like this, heat was a friend.

He had burned most of the kinetic energy in his flight but still had enough to make one of the mountains a pile of rubble if he needed to.

But he wouldn't. He had been working on precision lately. Now instead of killing everything in the room, he could just kill the particular nuisance of his choice.

Passing through the township (one seemed to form on the outskirts of every kingdom) was an exercise in endurance. Shops and stands were set up in neat concentric crescents around the castle keep with clear, uncluttered roadways and a massive boulevard cutting straight through, leading directly to keep's front door.

The people were fit, used to a life of toil and labor. They all had similar hair color, obviously from the same stock. Not a lot of variety in the bloodline, Shefa figured. They could be considered attractive, in a strong, hostile, built-for-breeding sort of way. It showed, even through the grime stains worked into their skin.

Stands sold fruits and vegetables in odd purples and deep oranges, bulbous things that might have been akin to a gourd from back home. Their language was soft and rolling with hard sounds that punctuated the ends of sentences, like the highborn dwarves of old. Completely different from AlinTown. It was beautiful in its own way.

Of all the strangeness assaulting him as he walked the long road to the castle, it was the smell that demanded his attention. Humans largely smelled the same with slight variations due to water source and diet, but this placed smelled old ... lost, like it was in a far-gone age, not the modern world of clean water and cooked meat. He blocked out what he could and took longer steps.

There were looks, of course; wearing all blacks and greys drew attention in a place where everything existed in shades of brown. He didn't take it personally.

It took nearly two hours to make it to the main keep, a high wall of red stone broken by a high arch and large guards. They wore armor made from the carapace of some monstrosity that likely only lived here, somewhere between a scorpion's back and a turtle's shell. They wore layers of the man-skirts they enjoyed in Silvetera, thick boots and helms that sat on the back of the skull, reaching around like the claw of a dragon. They stiffened at his approach.

"I am here to see the Kalmar," Shefa said in Elvish.

The guard on the left responded in the grunting that passed for speech in this land. Shefa raised his hands slowly while kneeling. He made a spectacle of praying, bowing his head to the earth then raising his face to the sky. A faint green glow permeated his flesh, gradually fading away to nothing.

In reality, he'd simply cast an illumination spell, but it always paid to lie to strangers. He stood.

"I am here to see the Kalmar."

The men's reactions were priceless as they deduced what the light show was for. To their credit, these men were professionals; they weren't shocked long.

"Leave," the blond on the left said.

"I am here to see the Kalmar," Shefa repeated.

The guards glanced at each other briefly. The redhead on the right spoke. "No one walks in and sees the Kalmar. Leave while you still can."

"I am a visiting dignitary. Is there not some protocol for when a king visits, even in this place?"

The guards weren't sure what to do.

"What is your business, *dockmar*?" Blondie asked.

Dockmar, Shefa mused.

He searched the large man's mind. *Mar* meant man. If the king were Kalmar, *kal* would be some variation of high, which would make *dock* some variation of low. Calling Shefa low was slightly less offensive than calling him ugly or drawing your sword, both of which required he break something precious to you, usually a rib.

Shefa took six short steps forward, bringing himself close enough to smell the man's breath. He craned his neck to look the man in the face. The large man looked down, half amused, half tense. Shefa looked at his friend. He slowly raised an open palm and casually shoved the man a dozen feet before he hit the ground, slid, rolled, and came to a wheezing stop against a pile of firewood stacked neatly next to the main gate.

The redhead was stunned. He'd just watched his fellow guardsman sail through the air like a small child. He winced when he hit the ground and began his unceremonious tumble-slide. He leveled his weapon, a beautiful affair, falling effortlessly into a fighting stance.

"I am here to see the Kalmar. Will you collect your superior or will I have to build a pile of fools to garner an appointment?" Shefa asked, nothing moving but his lips, not even blinking.

The guard whistled a peculiar tone and a series of brutes trotted out, all holding the same glorious blade. The weapon was a three-foot staff with a bladed handguard, good for breaking a cheekbone or slicing a throat when the enemy got too close. One end was capped with a foot-long wasp-waist blade that could slice like a scimitar or stab like a spear; flawless choice. The other end was fixed with the ten-inch claw of a fearsome beast that had to be larger than a horse. One could slice, slash, stab, punch, hook and eviscerate, all with one light, quick weapon. Shefa had finally found something to admire in this half-frozen mud-pit.

A dozen men, armed and armored similarly enough to be family, pounded out confused and angry. *Apparently, that song doesn't get whistled often,* Shefa thought. They surrounded him, pointing their blades at his squishy bits with disturbing accuracy. Not many men can aim a blade right for your kidney at five feet.

If nothing else, they were well drilled. He was ordered to kneel; he obeyed. He was bound at the wrists and ankles, searched thoroughly and dragged off by his wrists.

As freezing mud collected in the crack of his ass, he was sure to get the name of the man doing the pulling: Dridden. They would talk later.

The dungeon was nicer than expected. He had seen a few in his time, and by comparison, this one was pretty nice. The piss buckets froze so their stench was present but not suffocating, like most prisons. There was enough room to lay out flat or pace if one wanted to; always a plus.

However, the red bricks made the place darker than necessary. Shefa couldn't help but feel the torches were working extra hard, thanks to some long dead designer's poor taste. Shefa had been compliant through his unnecessary dragging. He had learned to hate in silence for years without it losing any of its intensity. No need to rush when the venom didn't dilute.

He waited an hour then called for the guards. After five minutes of that, he bent the bars, slipped out, and bent them back. Other prisoners barked out pleas in their guttural tongue: "Free me," "I don't belong here," "Witch," all sorts of nonsense. Shefa searched for one *not* bitching.

An old man sat on his bench in silence, resigned to his fate. Thin and weathered like everyone else, though not to the same extent. He clearly was a fairly new arrival. He wore a sack with a head hole, but no armholes. His legs were crossed at the ankles, and he appeared to be meditating. Shefa knocked on the bars of his cell. He was many things, but he was not rude.

"Go away. I have nothing of value to say," the man responded without opening his eyes. His voice was harsh and uninviting, like the warriors who'd raised him.

Shefa fought down a smile. "What is your name?"

"Bendlin."

"What is your crime?"

"Speaking truth to power."

"Do you want to die?" Shefa asked. The man shrugged. "Do you want to live?" His left eye peeled open. "Tell me Bendlin, do you know these walls?"

"I do. Served here twenty-four summer storms."

"I am in need of a guide, but I have no money. I am prepared to give you your life back if you will escort me to the throne room."

Bendlin squinted and cocked his head sideways. He knew what he was hearing was madness but there was no doubt, no fear in this strange man's eyes, eyes that glittered even in dungeon light. Dragon's eyes.

"What is *your* name?"

"Shefa DragonPaw, first of the Chimera, eldest of the emerald mistress, Emmafuumindall, king of all Fuumashon."

"What do you want with my Kalmar?"

"To kill the AlinGuard bandits for him."

"What is your crime?"

"I broke a guard," Shefa said with a smirk.

Bendlin smirked in return. "Do you want to die, king of all Fuumashon?"

"Not yet."

"Do you want to live?"

"More than any other to ever breathe."

"Free me from this cell, get me beyond the Polyphyodont, and I will take you to the Kalmar myself."

Shefa extended his hand through the bars, an offer to shake as the humans did in Silvetera, but Bendlin had no idea what to do. "In my homeland, we shake hands; a symbol of honesty and trust."

Bendlin smirked as he rose to his feet. "We do the same here. I just don't trust you."

A howling laughter burst from the Chimera, surprising himself as much anyone else. He placed his hands and heaved. The bars shrieked in resistance then bowed in compliance. Bendlin slipped his hand out from under his head hole sack and extended it. They grasped forearms, a soldier's greeting, bending forward until their foreheads kissed.

"Now, I trust you."

Shefa didn't want to, but he couldn't suppress it and smiled.

3

KING SHEFA KALMAR

Allow me to introduce myself, my name is...

Kalmar Grond sat atop his throne of Pilan, a purple wood that only grew in the Whitelands. It was as tall and imposing as one would expect from the king of a frozen wasteland. He waited impatiently, tapping his finger. The heavy gold ring he wore made a very particular noise as it clacked against the deep-froze wood of the chair. The sound was more of breaking ice than metal on wood. The process of deep-freezing ensured the throne would not succumb to the harsh climate, but all the same, a curious thing.

A runner told him minutes before that a prisoner had escaped and was making his way to the throne room. Guards had been placed at the door. A squad was sent to stop him long before he ascended the seven levels between the dungeon and the Kalmar'skeep. Based on the rate and pitch of the screaming echoing down the halls, he assessed a single fighting unit wasn't enough.

His NUUK—royal guardsmen that fought with him in every war of his lifetime—surrounded the throne. To be NUUK was to be an elder prince, untouchable and often a royal pain in the ass.

The throne room doors required four men to operate, a defensive measure and show of wealth. They usually sat open but were closed per protocol once the runner arrived. They were latched and bolted while the Kalmar waited for the intruder's body to be laid at his feet. Around the door, twelve crossbowmen waited casually, fully expecting the lesser warriors to handle such a small problem.

They were all great warriors once, but since no one was fool enough to attack the Kalmar in his keep, their true purpose during peacetime was to project an image of power; they never saw actual combat.

The Kalmar watched and waited. The NUUK watched and waited. The hall went silent. The locking bar set across the massive doors began to vibrate. The sound of trembling metal echoed in the hollow silence of that enormous room. Everyone leaned in, curiosity over-ruling combat experience and common sense. The bar shook faster and faster. The rumble of metal on wood became a crescendo of a whine until it cracked, a smooth break down the center, separating the left from the right and effectively picking the world's biggest lock.

The door swung open smooth and evenly as though pulled by trained presenters at court. Crossbows snapped into position; one row kneeling, the row behind standing. The four NUUK flanking the Kalmar's throne leveled their weapons, ready to kill or die without thought or hesitation.

A familiar voice echoed from the hall beyond.

"Grond, Kalmar of AlinHall, son of Hrond, Master of Clans, Uniter of Tribes. First among all, in this, the bosom of the north! I, Bendlin verkFirelaid, announce the arrival of an honored guest!"

The NUUK bristled at the audacity of this fallen fool. Drummed of the throne room, stripped of all honor and titles, foolish enough to openly defy the Kalmar, *at court*, no less! Now, this?! Escape from prison and announcing an enemy, a possible spy and assassin into the Kalmar's keep itself. His friendship with the Kalmar spared him the blade before, but surely now he must die.

Bendlin stepped in from the hall. He had spent half his life in the leather and furs of the NUUK. He had been stripped of that honor.

Now he served another Kalmar, Shefa. Promoted to royal announcer, he wore a uniform befitting his station.

He and Shefa were of a similar build so his armor fit spectacularly. The black leather trimmed in platinum, royal crest of Fuumashon emblazoned on his chest, an emerald the size of his thumb in the middle of its face. His diagonal cut cape, snow white with emerald lining, made him glow against the muted red stones of the keep. His steel grey hair, combed back and to the right, returned some measure of his dignity to him. Freshly shaven, boots shined to a polish, and finally fed to satisfaction; this man was prepared to die if this creature he had put his faith in failed.

"Fire!" Grond shouted.

Twelve bolts streaked across the room. Sharp metallic twangs filled the otherwise silent chamber, echoing off stone and glass to create a cacophony of howling death. Bendlin straightened his back. If this was to be his end, so be it. He would die as he lived: on his feet, honor intact.

Ten feet before impact, the bolts stopped. They didn't slow or waver; they stopped, hung still in midair as if they had never been moving. The clatter when they hit the stone floor was the most majestic sound the old warrior had ever heard. Bendlin blew out the most stress-filled breath he had ever held.

The guards looked to each other, then to their Kalmar, eyes wide, mouths open, hoping for any sign of instruction. They found none. Bendlin bowed, long and low, his faith in his new lord rock solid. He rose with a flourish.

"His majesty, Shefa DragonPaw, firstborn of the emerald mistress..."

"Em-ma-FUU-min-Dall," Shefa whispered from beyond the doorway.

"Emmafuumindall. Kalmar of all Fuumashon, future king of all the world. He has come requesting an audience, my lord."

Bendlin finished and stood, arms folded neatly behind him, breathing so shallow it appeared he held it. A soldier at attention was authorized to blink and breathe. Bendlin was a spectacular soldier. Five heartbeats passed before the Kalmar spoke.

"Bendlin. You were my friend since first we met in KruthDalar as whelps. I thought of you as my brother, as I do all my NUUK. It broke my heart to strip you, but you knew the price for losing the game you played. You chose your fate and I did my duty as Kalmar. But as your friend, I spared you. Now you betray me again." Kalmar's fingers gripped the arms of his throne, his right foot bouncing on tiptoe.

"It was my duty as your friend, brother, and NUUK to give you my counsel whether you wanted it or not. I said what I said, and I meant every word. I hold nothing but love for you in my heart and bear you no ill will. But you have proven yourself unfit and so I serve another," Bendlin responded, putting on a brave face but hurt, true emotional turmoil, raged just beneath the surface.

Kalmar Grond leaped to his feet. "She is my wife!"

"She is your ruin!" Bendlin shouted back with equal venom.

TWANG! The sound grabbed everyone's attention. Eyes turned, frantic. Grollick still held his crossbow leveled at Bendlin's heart. The bolt hovered a hand's length from Bendlin's chest. Grollick's aim was perfect. That emerald in the center of his armor pulsed, stealing the momentum from the missile as it approached.

With its work done, the gem fell dull and the bolt followed to the floor. Grond looked at Grollick with wide, vein-filled eyes. His teeth were visible through the part in his illustrious black beard as he scowled something vile at his First NUUK, Bendlin's replacement.

The Kalmar marched from his throne, his cape floating on the breeze of his rage. Grollick lowered his weapon, eyes weeping fear, but he stood his ground. Kalmar Grond punched Grollick in such a manner that no one watching expected him to survive. Grond turned back to Bendlin, marching with the same violent gait. Shefa coughed from the hall, reminding everyone he was still there. Grond stopped. He eyed Bendlin dangerously.

"Why have you brought this *dockmar* to my throne?" the Kalmar ground out through stress-creaking teeth.

"I have served you all my life. Here and now, I served you still."

Grond marched over to Bendlin, towering over him, his shoulders rising and falling with each tremoring breath. "What does he want?"

"To rid your steadhold of the fiends of AlinGuard."

Grond looked to the empty doorway. "Bring him. The instant I don't care for his words, he dies, you watch, and then you die."

"Of course, Kalmar," Bendlin said with a bow.

Bendlin took four steps back, turned about and marched out of the throne room. His boots clicked on the stone, the only sound in the massive room.

Grond ordered his men, "Secure the prisoner and prepare him for audience."

The men snapped a salute and disappeared into the hall. Several minutes passed. The sound the Kalmar's ring against his throne echoed in the empty room, keeping time as his orders were carried out.

An intermittent squeak came from the hall. Squeak ... squeak ... squeak... an upright cart came around the corner, wheel squeaking with every full rotation. Shefa seemed strangely at ease. He was chained to the cart: across the shins, waist, and throat. His ankles were chained together, as were his wrists, both also chained to the cart. A black hood was cinched tight over his head, tied with a braided leather strand around his neck. He wore no other clothing.

Six guards accompanied him, their strange deadly blades tracking perfectly with his vital organs. Dridden wheeled him along, coming to a stop ten paces before the Kalmar. As he brought him to a stop, he "accidentally" tipped him too far forward and Shefa pitched, ever so slowly, and landed on the stone face first.

There was a chuckle as the men straightened him out. The Kalmar didn't laugh. Shefa didn't laugh. Dridden caught his Kalmar's eye just long enough to let him know that not only was it *not* an accident, it wasn't the last one he would have as their guest.

"You come into my steadhold unannounced. Trespassing is punishable by death at my pleasure. You assault my guard and my nephew, both treason, both punishable by death at my pleasure. A good man has put his life on the butcher's block for you to say whatever you have come to say. Choose your words carefully; the first one I dislike is your last. Do you understand, *dockmar?*" the Kalmar explained.

The hood nodded. The Kalmar ripped it off. Wet sheep dung tumbled out as it came free. Shit and straw stuck to Shefa's hair and face. His nose bled freely from the fall. The guards and NUUK laughed again. If Shefa was affected, it didn't show.

Shefa opened his mouth and mumbled something unintelligible. The Kalmar leaned in, curious. Shefa mumbled again. The Kalmar sighed exasperatedly then looked around at his men. Dridden grinned stupidly.

The Kalmar shoved his gnarled, scarred fingers into Shefa's mouth and pulled out a footlong, piss-soaked rag. The men stifled a laugh. Shefa started to spit but decided that would be in poor taste in another's throne room. Instead, he chose to swallow the refuse in his mouth. He did what he could to bow.

"Kalmar. I am unfamiliar with your customs; if any offense is given, it is unintentional and I apologize one thousand times. Forgive me my transgressions."

"My son has treated you poorly; for this, I will double my tolerance and grant you a full minute of my time. What do you want, stranger?"

"Shefa. We have no Kalmar in my homeland."

Grond huffed, but he nodded. He would call this *dockmar* by his title, no matter how stupid it was. "Shefa. I am not patient. What?"

"You have a bandit problem. Tell me what you know of these bandits and the fortress they call home so that I may kill them for you."

"No."

Shefa waited. And waited. And waited some more. Eventually, he realized the man was counting down his promised minute.

"As Shefa, it is my duty to protect my people. Sadly, I know little about the world beyond my borders. One monarch to another, help me help my people. Teach me."

"No."

Frustrated, Shefa looked at the man, truly studied him. He was better than seven feet tall, a two-legged bear. Easily five-hundred pounds. He wore blood red leather, weaved in a design Shefa had never seen before, interlocking laces pulled into a smooth whole as singular as any wool shirt. Black leather pants, ankles trimmed in red fur. A bear's head flanked by howling wolves crest holding his half cape, itself lined in the same red fur.

This was wealth in these lands. His eyes were the pale blue of old ice. Long healed scars marked his cheeks, what little showed above his truly noteworthy beard. His crown, open jaws of some meat-eating predator, dipped in iron and polished hard enough to reflect the red of the stone that surrounded them.

"About ten seconds left?" Shefa asked.

"Less."

"Good. As a courtesy, I came to see you. Monarch to monarch. I am going to AlinGuard. I will deal with these bandits, then I will deal with that *SHIK-Lar* you call a son. You can tell me what you know, all that may be of use to me, or when I'm done with them and him, I will set my sights on you. We are men of action. We both know what that means."

The Kalmar narrowed his eyes. "One minute. Promise kept." He spun on his heels, marching for his throne. "Seize the traitor. Hand me my Axis."

"AXIS! That's what it's called!" Shefa said with the glee that flows from finally scratching a hard to reach itch.

Men moved toward Bendlin, Axis' ripe for bloodletting.

"If you touch him, I will take all of your teeth, one at a time." The men paused at the bizarre threat. "If you harm him, you will die weeping in this very room."

Shefa's voice wasn't loud or threatening. He spoke as though he were telling them that rain falls from the sky, the simplest and most commonly known fact. That is what made it so threatening. They shook off the threat and went back to their task.

Shefa summoned the kinetic energy stored in his flesh and bled it into the chains securing him. Wave after wave of violent energy filled the spaces between the molecules until the metal vibrated with a haunting metallic jingle. With a slight flex of his muscles, he jangled the chains, starting a chain reaction. The superfluous energy, desperate for a path of escape, blew the wood and metal apart with a deafening retort.

Wood went from ash to smoke so fast not a single burning ember touched the ground. The overpressure from the explosion knocked every man in the room on his ass. Metal streaked out across the room, molten ore that clung to and burned everything it touched. Men screamed as naked flesh was peppered with bubbling iron.

Bendlin, dressed in Shefa's inertia-dampening armor was protected from the blast but he was still rocked by the explosion. Instinct had him crouch in fear from the sheer volume of sound thundering off the stone. Shefa stood among the swirling smoke and scorch marks, charred skin already healing, eyes glowing a shade of green that could only be interpreted as wicked. He searched the room for just a fraction of a second before finding his prize.

Dridden was climbing to his feet. He and Shefa had unfinished business and a king should always pay his debts. He marched over to the man who was still on hands and knees, shaking his head as though it might help him focus. Shefa stomped on the back of his head, sandwiching it between scale hard skin and stone hard floor. The man slumped concernedly still, face on the floor, ass in the air.

"Stay," was all he said. He leaped thirty feet, landing like a cat, within arm's reach of Bendlin. "Are you well?"

Bendlin looked at him in stunned silence.

"Bendlin?"

"I am well, my lord."

"Did they touch you?"

"I'm sorry?"

"Which of these chamber pot stains shall I kill first?"

Bendlin looked at these men; all of them had been his brothers longer than they hadn't. He didn't want to see harm come to any of them.

"No, my lord. None touched me."

"Shefa. It is my title, but it is also my name. No more 'my lord,' yes?"

"Yes—" he caught himself before he said "my lord" again.

Shefa nodded. "When you were NUUK, did you have an Axis?"

"I did. All NUUK are awarded one of glass-steel and deep-froze wood upon indoctrination to the order."

"Do you still have it?"

Bendlin shook his head. "It was stripped from me along with my rank and title."

Shefa reached out his hand toward the throne where Grond's Axis Scepter had landed after the explosion. The gorgeous weapon, trimmed in flowing strips of hide from all the beasts he had slayed, jumped across the empty space, slapping into his waiting hand. Shefa twirled it once and handed it to the man.

"Your replacement."

The room was on its feet now. The NUUK carried Axis Primes; instead of a foot-long blade and ten-inch claw fastened to a three-foot staff, they swung a five-foot staff with a two-foot blade and a claw large enough to hook a man around the waist. Several were aimed at the southern dragon. The men holding them were eager for his blood.

Shefa was born and bred for this. Shefa had wet dreams about this. Shefa suppressed a shiver of pleasure and did his god's work.

The nearest man made a mini-slice, nearly too quick to see and certainly too quick to avoid. It was a short swipe meant to open his throat and leave him on the floor, clawing at the stone for a breath that would never come.

Shefa leaned back while stepping forward, taking his throat out of range of the weapon but bringing him in danger close behind it. There was the briefest sliver of a moment for the man to panic. Shefa grabbed him under the arms and launched him skyward. The man would soar five times his height, screaming and flailing his arms before shattering both his legs. Shefa didn't bother to watch; he had seen this show many times before.

Before the man on his right could move, the dragon kicked him in the chest. Not hard enough to penetrate his shell armor, but hard enough shoot him like a lake skipped stone across the keep floor until something too hard to give stopped him.

A step forward brought him between two men, ready and on their guard. He raised a palm to each, releasing invisible blasts of pure kinetic force. The thing about *kin* is it didn't affect the surface of things like normal energy. It would not crumple one side of a box while leaving the other untouched.

When *kin* struck, it permeated an object, affecting each molecule. The men weren't stuck with a hammer's worth of force to the face;

that hammer hit every fiber of their skulls with equal force in the exact same instant.

They were pulled, as if by charging horses, off their feet by their heads. Necks made a wet, sickening sound as they simply went elsewhere. Shefa looked back at Bendlin. The man gave him a terrified curt nod, which his Shefa returned with equal brevity. Shefa scanned the room. Six men and the Kalmar stood against him. His point had been made. He just wanted his pants now.

"Stand down. Dridden still owes me a debt, but there is no reason for the rest of you to be hobbled."

The dragon's voice was frighteningly calm. He stood naked and weaponless yet in complete comfort. It made the Kalmar's blood run cold. How many men had this stranger broken and not even bother to bury? How much blood had he bathed in simply for the sport of it? But he would not be cowed.

"I am still Kalmar here! There are no orders but my own!" the fool roared with a charge.

"Protect the Kalmar!" some smaller fool screamed, and his men rushed to beat him to their foe.

Shefa closed his eyes, opened his hands and found the kinetic energy emanating from their charge. And cut it. The seven of them simply stopped. One fool fell over, unprepared to be suddenly standing instead of moving. They looked around confused, as still as if they had never started running.

"I came here to serve. To help you with a problem undercutting your authority and stealing the lives of your subjects; men, women, and children under your protection," the dragon said.

The Kalmar bristled but did nothing else.

Shefa began a slow walk forward. "I can kill you all, without effort or consequence. I doubt I would even remember your screams a week from now. But I have not come as an enemy, or a conqueror. I came to serve. Fool."

The Kalmar stood his ground. His massive frame towered over the dragon in human flesh. Shefa looked up at the man whose arm was bigger around than his waist. There was no fear in his eyes. He would not be shamed here. He would not show weakness. Here, in the halls of his ancestors and the promise to offspring, he was Kalmar. He had lived that way and despite the challenge that stood before him, he would die that way.

"Bendlin is coming with me. This is not a request. Dridden will be my guide into AlinGuard. I will return him in working order if it is within my power. Now tell me what it is I face, or I will cripple you and give your throne to the first fool who will have it, lineage be damned. So, Kalmar, Grond. Choose."

4

THE WICKED PASS

"Show me the wonders of your land, and I will show you mine. Feminine flower to bloody blade."

The Wicked Pass was misnamed, Shefa thought, as horses fit for giants carried them through the Polyphyodont Mountains. Dridden was pissed about his father agreeing to send him to his death and he wore his contempt openly. Shefa and Bendlin rode in silence, neither enjoying the day nor lamenting the journey.

Warriors had a way of simply being, allowing no thoughts to enter their mind while simultaneously staying completely prepared to kill. The pass was little more than a break in the mountains, as if the force that made the monuments to the left and right had ran out of steam when it got to this bit.

As if they'd hit some invisible barrier, the horses at once, threw a fit. Whatever means employed, they would not take a single step forward.

"Far as we go," Bendlin said, dismounting.

The horses were weighed down with a week's worth of supplies for the two men. It appeared Shefa was planning to starve to death if he lived that long.

Granted access to whatever they might need from the Kalmar, Bendlin retrieved the armor and weapon he knew and loved best. He looked odd to Shefa in red leather and scorpion shell, but then he had only seen the man in his own armor and a dirty sack.

"The horses will travel no further. These dumb beasts have more brains than you," Dridden mocked Shefa.

"More than you, as well," Shefa responded.

Dridden scoffed. "This isn't my head-empty plan, *dockmar*."

"No, but the horses can leave. You are enslaved. Seems to me they made better life choices than you. Either they are smart for horses, or you're dumb by any measure."

Shefa delivered his speech no with no anger or venom. He stated it as clear irrefutable fact, which only made it sting more. Dridden shut his mouth and went about the business of unpacking his horse in angry silence.

When the horses were unpacked and Bendlin's camp was set up, Shefa approached Dridden who stiffened in response.

"Calm, boy; if I were gonna hurt you, I wouldn't have dragged you out here to do it."

"I don't fear you."

"Then I insulted the horses by comparing your intelligence."

Dridden thought for a moment, processing the words carefully, then again before the insult revealed itself to him. His eyes widened and reddened as veins bulged in his neck and arms. He was on the verge of a murderous rage, barely kept in check, by what, Shefa didn't know. He sighed in the larger man's face.

"Find something useful to do with your rage, you overgrown angry toddler."

Dridden threw a right cross with all the muscles of his chest, arm, legs,and back. Shefa stood fast as the blow approached. A meaty fist, filled with battle-hardened bones, tempered in war and the harshest climate, slammed into his face with a smack that echoed off the valley beyond. Dridden dropped to his knees, cradling his broken fist in his quivering hand.

"I am Chimera, you stupid little man. My mother was a dragon. My bones are hard as iron. Normally, I would kill you and be done with it.

Fools bore me over-quickly. But you, stupid son of a stupid king, someday people will live or die based on that soft puddle of goat shit between your ears. So, you will learn on this trip, or you will prove to me that you cannot learn and *I will* kill you, for the sake of all those who would follow your shit-brained lead. Is that simple enough for you to follow?"

The broken prince nodded, sucking and blowing air through clenched teeth as he struggled to retain his pride and dignity, though neither really existed at this point. Shefa cradled the man's hand. He pulled away, out of fear, in a pitiful attempt at protection. Shefa took his hand as though no resistance ever existed. He summoned pulsing waves of healing energy, watching and listening as bones healed and popped back into place.

When he released him, the prince could only stare in amazement. Magic was well known, even at the top of the world, but it was only authorized for use by agents of the emperor and only by express written permission. Violation called down the wrath of the Silver Shades and NO ONE, man, beast, or mythical creature, wanted a date with a Silver Shade.

"Don't worry. This is my kingdom and I do as I please," Shefa said, interpreting the man's fears. He had heard them all before. "We eat, then we march."

Dridden nodded, short and smart.

Dridden hefted his shield and followed the King of Fools through the Wicked Pass. Shefa hadn't seen an AlinHold shield before. It was the shape of a cat's eye, pointed on both ends. Large enough to cover a man's torso. It too was the shell of some dream-haunting creature, and this one was painted in what Shefa guessed was a family crest or some shit. It looked heavy. Shefa liked heavy.

They climbed a steep grade of hard packed ice that took half an hour to crest. At the top, they could see the infamous AlinGuard. It sucked.

"You look like you've seen a ghost," Dridden said with a chuckle.

Shefa turned his head slowly. He looked at Dridden's smirking face with an expression the mocking man couldn't quite place. Shefa relaxed his eyes, pulled his ears back and turned the corners of his mouth up ever-so-slightly.

"This is my 'seen a ghost' face, see. It's different."

Dridden wasn't sure if it was a joke or if this fool was fully maddened. Shefa smirked to himself.

"So, turn back?" Dridden asked, sure the man clearly saw the folly of his ways.

"Back? No. Here is fine," Shefa answered.

Dridden's face scrunched up in confusion. Shefa went into the small bag he kept strapped to his chest. He pulled out a ring, a plain iron band with a touch of rust, capped by a small turquoise stone. He slipped it on his first finger. The only other thing in the bag was a gem the size of an apple.

Dridden's eyes went tear-at-the-corners wide at the sparkling pink stone. Shefa took it in an underhand gasp, spun his arm three times, gaining speed and power with each revolution, and whipped it into the sky. Dridden watched it until it disappeared from view.

"You threw it away?"

"Keep looking," Shefa said, folding the bag carefully.

A heartbeat later, the stone exploded in a glorious display of racing waves of glittering pink that covered most of the visible sky. The sound hit the ground hard enough to roll the snow and bend the hair in the Northman's nose. The display hung around for a minute, maybe more, and then faded to nothing. Dridden looked to Shefa who was taking off his armor. He started to ask what he was doing but decided to just watch instead.

Topless, bootless, and working off his pants, the southerner seemed to be growing more foolish by the second. A strange sizzle hit the air behind them. Dridden spun, Axis at the ready.

A purple portal cut a hole in space and the strangest man the prince had ever seen stepped through. He was a head shorter than the Northman but well built. Long black hair, a starter beard, and girlish look about him; Dridden hated him instantly. Shefa was down to his loin wrap at this point, completely unaware of the stranger's presence.

No, he realized, this man was summoned. THE CRYSTAL! It all made sense now. Still, the ice warrior kept his blade trained on the new arrival.

"Do you have my bag?" Shefa asked, peeling off his stained loin wrap as if he weren't standing ankle-deep in snow. He looked up and seemed genuinely surprised. "Did they not see the beacon?" he asked, a bit irritated.

The stranger showed no sign of fear. "You asked for help. Help is here," the man said with an elaborate mock bow. Shefa made a face that said "unimpressed." Clearly, they were friends. Maybe equals.

Gods, are there more of him? Dridden thought.

With a flick of his wrist, Shefa burned his stained underwear and tossed them aside where they continued to burn in the snow.

"This is a big job," he said, flexing his fingers hungrily as though the bag he requested held his child.

The new guy unslung a black bag from his shoulder and tossed it. Shefa caught it and opened it with more emotion than Dridden had seen from him thus far.

"Mim has king stuff. Patience is making it harder. The council is ... the council, and Gala is smashing heads in the south."

"He *does* love smashing heads," Shefa said with a warm half-smile. "So, Alexandrite?"

"Yay," they said simultaneously and did a silly dance with their hands.

Dridden screwed up his face like he'd smelled a fart he didn't hear. "What the frozen hell is going on here?!" the prince barked. Neither man responded. Dridden, furious, drew in a sharp breath.

"Can I kill him?" the new guy asked Shefa, shocking and sending Dridden into a coughing fit.

Shefa looked at him then and seemed to be weighing his options. "No. He's a prince," he finally said.

"Ah," the man said, seeming disappointed. "Greetings, prince. I am

Rorou Albright of Fuumindall's Horn," he said, adding a genuine if shallow bow. "My king here seems to have a terrible idea in his head and it appears he's dragging you along for the festivities. Am I close?"

This man was dangerous. He didn't look it but every body hair Dridden had was standing on end, some very uncomfortably. He wore a tight shirt made of a cloth the Northman had never seen. It was purple of all things! Thick brown pants, heavy, and I mean *heavy*, boots. A dagger strapped to his chest was the only weapon the prince could see which meant the man was crazy or didn't need any.

It took a minute for him to realize Rorou was actually waiting for an answer.

"Uh, yeah. Your friend wants to die."

Rorou laughed. It was a beautiful tinkling sound that the wind couldn't diminish though it tried. This Rorou was lighthearted and pleasant. A tad feminine by northern standards but his eyes were terrifying. There was nothing, *absolutely nothing* behind them. No thoughts, no soul, no person. And when he smiled, it got worse.

"Did you hear that? We're friends," Rorou said, not quite mockingly, but as if he were humoring a small child. "My dear prince..."

He waited. Dridden waited. They both waited. Shefa waited for them to finish waiting but they waited more, harder somehow.

"What is your name, Prince?"

"Oh! Dridden!"

Rorou recoiled as if he'd smelled something foul. "Well, we can't pick our own names. Prince Dridden, Shefa is not my friend; he is my king. It's the only reason I haven't killed him," Rorou explained, and his hollow malicious eyes called him true.

"That, and you can't," Shefa said from behind, wrapping on a new loincloth.

"And I can't," Rorou admitted. "So, unfortunate prince, what circle of Hell does my king wish to plummet to today?"

Dridden thought hard, processing every big complicated word before he spoke. "He wants to go to AlinGuard."

"And what the hell is AlinGuard?"

"AlinGuard Prison!"

"AlinGuard ... prison?"

"Yes."

"Prison for what? Devils, demons, monsters from Hell, champions from Heaven, elementals who feel no pain?"

Dridden saw more than a rambling of words here. This man *expected* more than AlinGuard Prison. This wasn't a list of his fears; this was his wish list!

"Neither of you ever heard of AlinGuard?!" the prince asked incredulously.

Shefa jumped in. "It's like the Mind's Eye Temple," he said, casually slipping on tight black pants. They looked to be made of spider silk.

"Oooh! You found another funhouse!" Rorou said with what seemed like barely suppressed glee. "Is it as bad as Azreal's Tower?"

"The locals seem to think so."

"Any talent up here?"

"Some good fighters, but no Jewels."

"Hmmph," Rorou said. What it meant, Dridden couldn't be sure. "Prince! Show me!" Salivation poured through those evil orbs in his eye sockets.

Dridden led him over the crest to where he could clearly see the prison and he swore the man's breathing increased like he was in one of the whore houses in AlinHall. Rorou turned to Dridden; his smile was the devil's.

"*This* ... will be fun!"

BUT, WHY?

"Men create because they can, never stopping to ask if they should. Never make what you cannot unmake."

Bendlin had made his camp, stripped his armor, and started preparing lunch when the Chimera and the prince came back down the mountain. Rorou insisted he needed a guide. Shefa agreed.

Ben was not happy about it, but the look in their eyes left very little room for debate. A younger man would have had questions; why, what about the horses, who the hell is that guy, where did he come from? Bendlin had served power all his life. He packed up and fell in line.

"I fear I will be of limited use to you," Bendlin said.

"Limited will be more than enough," Rorou charmed back.

They moved in silence as they climbed the hill. The only sounds? The ever-howling wind and the crunch of ice underfoot. When they reached the peak, all of them sighed.

"Prince, what am I looking at?" Shefa asked.

Dridden looked confused. "AlinGuard. I have told you this before, don't you remember?"

Bendlin huffed. "AlinGuard is a prison fortress built from a Dwarven stronghold seated in a frozen valley surrounded by seven layers of defense."

Shefa nodded. "Go on."

"From east to west the compound spans four *TANS*—"

"What is a *TAN*?" the Chimera said in unison.

Bendlin thought for a moment. "A unit of distance. Um ... a good horse can travel twenty *TANS* a day if that helps," he said, looking lost yet hopeful.

"Three-fifths of a league," Rorou said, having always been better at math than Shefa. Shefa still looked unsure. "A mile. That monster is a mile wide," Rorou clarified. Shefa nodded.

"Continue?"

"Please."

"One central hold, roughly the size of a village. Six full keeps, each with four prison towers and three archer towers. The entire compound is surrounded by a moat, home to some nasty burrowing creatures and, of course, placed on the highest, coldest plateau this frozen wasteland has to offer."

"AlinGuard is inescapable," Dridden said, turning all heads.

Rorou grinned sadistically. "That's why they didn't bother trying. Why escape? Just kill the guards and make the place home. It's what I would've done." He looked to Shefa who was already nodding.

Dridden shook his head. "Mad. All of you."

"Yes," the Chimera said in unison.

Down the slope at the mouth of the dale sat a wide-open plain Bendlin referred to as the Grave.

"Why do they call it the Grave?" Rorou asked.

"Those who attempt to escape and fail, which is all of them, are reanimated as living corpses, doomed to wander that stretch of land 'til the end of time."

"So what?" Rorou asked with genuine flummuxation.

"*So what?!*" Dridden roared. "They are cursed! Souls trapped here, never to join their ancestors in the higher halls! Do you Greenland fools know nothing?!"

He was blowing great gouts of steaming breath into the frozen air, shoulders heaving with each melodramatic breath. Shefa turned to the man and stared intensely at his angry face. Dridden didn't back down from the glare.

Shefa poked the large Northman in the eye. "Chapped lips shouldn't distress a *man* below the waist. Adjust."

Dridden hid his embarrassed blush behind his large hands and continued to rub his eye long after it stopped hurting.

"Let's get this over with," Shefa said and started forward.

"My Shefa. There are more dangers," Bendlin blurted.

"Just Shefa. Tell me on the way."

Around the clearing stood dead, sick-looking trees. Black sticks scratched on a white canvas, gnarled, twisted branches stabbing out in hooks, reached toward the ground rather than for the sun. As they got closer, he could see there were scores of strange birds perched in them. They gave off a dark, hostile aura. Shefa scowled; Rorou smiled.

"Birds? In the snow? God this place is awful."

"Not birds. Bleeders. Giant bloodsuckers. They prevent anyone from running ... for long."

"Dead men and bats? *This* is supposed to stop the best of the worst? Everything is relative, I guess," Rorou said with clear frustration.

Dridden huffed in mirrored frustration.

Rorou gave the man his attention. "Yes, your highness?"

"Dead men and bats? Is that what you think you see?"

"Do educate me. What *is* so scary about these ... defenses?"

Dridden shook his head and looked away. Rorou looked at Bendlin and Shefa; both shrugged.

Rorou decided to press. "Do the dead possess some power I'm

unaware of? Can they eat souls or control minds, or ... I don't know, something other than shuffle around and moan?"

It was then that Dridden realized for the first time that no, they couldn't really do more than that. They were dead. Slow. Falling apart. Why *was* he so afraid of them?

They pressed forward. As they stepped onto the prison grounds proper, the ice cracked under Shefa's foot, a sharp, clear clarion call that traveled farther and deeper than any natural sound ought to. High-pitched shrieks belted out from the shriveled black trees as hundreds of bleeders, mosquitos the size of ravens with thick leathery bat wings, burst to life and flooded the sky.

Shefa walked casually out into their midst, watching them absently, daring any to approach him. A scourge of the beasts descended. He raised a hand and released hellfire. Scores of crispy bodies tumbled from the sky. Dridden and Bendlin clutched their Axis', eyes wide, bodies tense. Shefa felt a small pang of pity for them. He crossed the ice, crunching water old as the stones beneath them. One more swarm tried its luck. Black corpses.

There was a clear path to the gaping doors of the prison, just less than a quarter mile away. Nothing but crypt silence and pure white broken only by more flakes of white falling and occasionally reflecting what passed for sunlight here. Two steps further and the sound of breaking ice popped up all around him. It was as if the very earth started hatching. Scores and scores and scores of stress marks broke the frozen floor as dead limbs reached up from beneath.

"VOldMoRTH!" Dridden shouted, warning the party.

Bendlin spun his Axis and set his feet, ready to die. Shefa lowered his head, summoning raw kinetic energy.

Rorou laid a hand on his shoulder. "Let's see what the Northmen are made of," he said with requesting eyes.

Shefa sighed. Together they watched as ice-blue skeletons, haphazardly dressed in scraps of meat, pulled themselves up and stalked forward. They shambled forward, screaming without lungs, stalking without eyes. Without warning, they charged, twice as fast as any living man could. Shefa cocked an eyebrow in surprise while Rorou burst into laughter.

Dridden howled. Bendlin howled. Monsters wailed and the battle for AlinGuard began.

Bendlin and Dridden took up defensive positions, back to back, and braced against the charge. Frigid bones raced forward, swiping sharp fleshless fingers with vile intent. Bright steel flashed as the Northmen hacked them down. They moved like well-casted pieces in a machine.

When Bendlin lunged, sliding his blade between rotting ribs to hold the thing in place, Dridden would swipe down through its collar bones, shattering ribs and spines. Skeletons collapsed in jagged heaps; the magic that animated them left with nothing of use.

Dridden would rush out and slash through neck bones, sending heads flying from the right while Bendlin would snap through shins from the left. They didn't speak. They didn't consult. They didn't miss. Together they moved in a zigzagging blur of red leather and throaty grunts.

When the bones piled up and cluttered the battlefield, they fell back exactly seven steps and started their dance from the top. The dead rushed forward, waves and waves of them blocking the way forward. The Northmen set their blades swinging; not to cut, but to cleave.

With crisp cracks, bones separated into useless chunks, leaving the monsters little more than angry wailing skull. They didn't bother to finish off those who clung to unlife; they simply moved on to the next. They were laying a carpet of bones atop the ice.

For ten minutes, the men battled the horde, never looking for help or escape, as if they had resigned themselves to dying on that very spot.

"End this," Shefa said to Rorou.

Rorou nodded, once, sharply.

He took off at a light jog, picking up speed. Reaching a full sprint, a strange purple-blue glow surrounded him, growing in intensity. The fray getting closer, scores of the undead encircling the Northerners; he leaped. In a poetic display, the iridescent glow warped, wrapping in, around, and over itself, taking the form of a hammer made of pure energy.

This was no reasonable hammer. The head was thirty-feet across, attached to a polearm twenty feet long. He pulled with every muscle in his body and brought it down like the wrath of God. A thousand bones were hammered down into the ice like nails, whatever animated them shattered in kind. Without a thought, he swung it around overhead, changing it into a great-sword thirty feet long.

He went through the remaining horde like a scythe. The sound of brittle bones shattering rattled out like morbid chimes. Fragments covered the yard, a rainbow of destruction following his slash. Shefa never moved any closer. He closed his eyes, summoned and released an orb of raw, explosive power in the center of the remaining skeletal formation. The explosion echoed off the mountains, creating an echo chamber of noise that lasted an eternity.

Dridden and Bendlin looked around stunned, chests heaving with anxious breaths. Wide, wild eyes scanned the area, finding only twitching bones and pools of warm water, already starting to refreeze.

"Why didn't you do that from the beginning?!" Dridden screamed at him across the yard.

"I wanted to see what you could do," Rorou answered, walking over to the pair, seeming very pleased with himself.

While Shefa walked over, Rorou picked bone slivers out of his hair and clothes. Bendlin leaned on his Axis, trying to catch his breath. Dridden was on the verge of a rage. Shefa walked up to him and touched the man's forehead.

"Calm."

All the anger flooded out of the man.

"What did you do?" the prince asked, baffled.

"Helped. What comes next?" Shefa asked, but Bendlin was not yet in a position to answer.

He pulled the turquoise stone ring off the middle finger of his right hand and shoved it onto the old man's finger. Bendlin was flooded with a stinging energy. He felt wounds decades old blaze fire-hot and fade away a second later. Broken bones that had healed poorly years ago reset themselves.

The ever-present tightness in his back lessened and the fluid that pooled in his lungs over a lifetime of breathing heavy air, drained, leaving breathing easier than any time he could remember. The whole affair took less than five minutes. He spun on Shefa with an unmistakable awe in his eyes.

"This is how you feel all the time?!"

"More or less," Shefa said with a disinterested shrug. "Roo. Get ready to make a path."

Rorou threw Shefa a salute so casual it seemed in jest. Shefa turned back to find Bendlin staring at him.

"Yes?"

"I cannot accept this. What kind of subject would I be if I deprived my lord of such a tool?"

Shefa noticed he did not unfinger the ring. He smirked. He liked this man; he was no fool. Shefa was a walking arsenal. He wore two rings, standard issue for all Fuumashon soldiers. The Cyan ring, which increased stamina, cast nearly perpetual healing and cut the need to eat and drink more than in half. On his left hand, the Kinstone ring, set with Alexandrite and surrounded by rare purple diamonds, allowed him to store enough kinetic energy to turn a village into a crater.

The black silks he wore under his armor kept his temperature constant in both frigid cold and intense heat. His armor was fitted with Kinstones that absorbed kinetic energy, slowing all incoming objects. He still wore Garrison's boots, Quest and Journey, which would never let him tire while he wore them. The green and red sashes tied around each arm bent light around him, making him appear more than a foot to the left or right of his true position.

And of course, Suffer, his tool. A living chunk of deep purple metal that could change shape with a thought, making sure he always had the right tool for the job. To face the lord of Fuumashon was to face an army of killers. Few things in all the world were more foolish.

Shefa showed off his other ring and lied, "I have a spare." Without another thought he headed toward the forest of towers, calling back over his shoulder. "Roo!"

With a huff, Rorou gave his Cyan ring to Dridden and followed.

They passed through what was once a wrought iron fence and into the second section of the yard.

"They call this the Grinder," Bendlin said, looking at the patch of frost like his own tombstone.

"Oh, pray tell," Rorou chimed.

"Most fall to the gargoyles who guard the doors. The strongest make it to the Grave," he said, nodding to the area behind them. "But all who wish to escape have to make it through here, the Grinder."

Rorou took two steps forward. "And what can we expect from the Grinder?" he asked, way too excited about it all.

"Well, I've never seen it myself, but it goes Spikes make a home here. Burrowing creatures that sleep beneath the ice. They are drawn to heat and sound."

"Stepping on that ice is suicide," Dridden said.

"I'm famously difficult to kill," Rorou offered without tearing his eyes away.

Shefa summoned kinetic energy from the ever-howling wind and fired a beam that punched into the ice, startling the Northmen. He cut a line across the Grinder. Crackling ice barked in a leaping staccato song that echoed across the tundra. A heartbeat of tense silence passed before dozens of monsters leaped from the ice like hungry fish.

They shot up and dived in beautiful arcs, mouths full of triangle teeth snapping every inch of the way. They were as long as an average man, white as the ice they lived beneath, earthworms thick as wolves with a glowing hot horn atop their heads. They hit the ice and wriggled for a moment before melting and digging a hole and disappearing.

"Well, that shouldn't be much of a problem," Rorou said, sounding disappointed.

"Roo, it's cold."

"Fine."

Rorou closed his eyes and touched the tips of his fingers together. From his feet, a swirl of bluish-purple energy (a color he dubbed "purble") formed at his feet. A moment later, it spread into a thin line, ten feet long and from that line, a bridge seemed to grow out of the ice. It was a simple affair, a thin band of energy that arched gently from his feet to the gate on the far side of the field.

"I'm sure it looks easy but this takes quite a bit of focus, so if we could move it along..."

Rorou bade the Northmen. They moved onto the bridge, tapping with their feet to test its sturdiness.

"It'll hold; move your asses!" Rorou barked, for the first time showing an emotion other than lust.

They piled onto the bridge, moving swift and sure, seemingly more afraid of it collapsing halfway across than actually reaching the other side. When the Northerners cleared the bridge, they looked back to find the Chimera hadn't moved. Dridden scowled fiercely, fearing they had been set up. Shefa made a stirrup by interlacing his fingers. Rorou stepped in.

With a grunt, Shefa heaved and the rugged elf shot up and over the field in the same arc as his bridge which was already fading into nothing. He landed like a butterfly with sore feet; there was barely even a disturbance in the ice. Shefa squatted and snarled as he launched himself to land beside his friend.

They looked back at the Grinder; the Northmen stunned, Shefa bored, Rorou crestfallen. They turned to face their goal, one more field, fifty more feet to the front door of AlinGuard. This close, Shefa could see the Dwarven craftsmanship in the lay of the stones, the sigils carved into every brick dampening all magic inside.

The lowest windows were thirty feet off the ground. They weren't made of glass but some other clear substance that seemed more like translucent honey or water that got stuck halfway to freezing.

"Gargoyles, yes?"

"Yes, my Shefa."

"Just Shefa."

All eyes turned up, scanning the building for the gargoyles purported to be the first obstacle to those trying to escape, the last for the invaders. A terrible ear-splitting howl ripped from the stone. It was no animal created by nature making that awful sound, Shefa knew that immediately.

From the stone, fever dream monsters from the mind of a devil worshiper slithered out like oil. Beasts as large as horses with the bodies of over-muscled hunting cats. They had the heads of bulls with a curved horn growing from the snout. Huge coiled ram's horns. Growing from between their shoulder blades was the torso of a man, covered in scales as thick as plate armor, dripping something dark that sizzled when it hit the snow.

The man-portion had arms too long for its body, covered in the same scales, ending in three-fingered oversized claws. Dragon-wings stretched out of the main body as bat wings flared from the humanoid. Each of the beasts had two tails; one ending in a boney spiked club, the other in a needle-sharp stinger, also dripping something that stunk even in the frozen breeze.

"Count," Shefa said.

Bendlin began counting the creatures as they pulled free of the stone. Dridden huffed like an amateur trying not to piss his pants.

"Twelve," Rorou said. "But how many more are lurking beneath the stone?"

"Bendlin, can we level the building?"

Bendlin looked at him as if he'd asked how heavy he thought the moon was. "Destroy thousand-year-old Dwarven Spellstone?" was all he could get out.

Shefa nodded; the question was ridiculous, he realized, after hearing it out loud. Shefa shook his head.

"*That's* what passes for gargoyles out here?"

Bendlin shrugged. "I've heard them called Mounted Riders if you like."

Shefa shrugged. "Better. Can we just run past them?" Shefa asked.

"If that door doesn't open, our backs are against the wall, Shefa. Not smart," Rorou advised.

Shefa sighed. "Have fun."

Rorou exploded into action. Two-ton monsters stampeded toward the lone Chimera as he raced toward them, fearless in his insanity.

"Bendlin, watch the left. Dridden, the right. Don't let them surprise us."

Shefa then started his slow march to help his clansman. Bendlin stood ready, his former prince at his back. He could feel the tension in the man.

"Your Highness?"

"NUUK."

Silence fell.

"I can feel the words rolling around in your head. It is a prince's prerogative to speak his mind."

"I'm not your prince anymore, remember? You serve a new master now."

"Ah," Bendlin said.

Dridden sighed. "And what is it you think you've figured out, old man?"

"You think me a traitor."

"I think you a coward."

Bendlin dropped his Axis, spun the prince around and slapped him hard across the face with his heavily gloved hand. Blood leaped out of the young man's mouth, a piece of tooth floating in the stream. Dridden wiped his mouth, stunned. He looked at the man who had stood by his father through countless campaigns.

He saw the coward who chose to serve a new master rather than obey his king as he had sworn, but he also saw the man who had taught him to ride a horse, string a bow, bed a woman. Conflicting emotions threatened to tear the young prince in half. He released a scream of frustration that was soundly interrupted by an even harder slap.

"I serve but do not think me a slave, boy. I watched you snatched out of your mother's hole and I spent my life teaching you what it means to be a man. For all the good it did. Look at you! Still the child who killed his brother because he was afraid he would be replaced."

Dridden stood, head held low but eyes burning with the urge to kill. "You swore your life to my father, OUR KALMAR! It was wrong, what he did to you, but you swore to *serve*!"

"So, I should die for a fool's pride?!"

"That fool is your Kalmar!"

"I will not die for a WHORE!"

The two men huffed at each other. Staring. Waiting. Watching. If either made a move, they were both resigned to fight to the death. Honor had been insulted. Names had been called. Egos had been bruised. In the north, satisfaction required blood. But neither moved. Bendlin turned to pick up his weapon, and Dridden mumbled something behind him.

"Yes, highness?" the old man asked, brimming for a fight.

"I said, you hit like a bitch."

"Your mother taught me."

Silence.

They burst into laughter.

Rorou was deathly serious. It was a rare sight. Shefa loved it. He rushed straight into the center of the enemy line. He constructed a long spear with a blade like a needle. As the Rider drew back, his too-long arms to swipe, the Mount lowered its head to gore him. Rorou dodged left at the last moment, flying into a sliding front split, and jabbed the Mount deep in the eye.

The beast wailed as it listed, the Rider's swipe missed. As the Mount plowed past, the clubbed tail smashed down. Rorou rolled just in time to escape the blow that created a geyser of stinging ice on impact and a thunder he felt in his chest. Rorou looked back. The Rider seemed to coddle the Mount as though they weren't one being.

The line continued forward toward Shefa who was still walking casually out to meet them. The Rider turned from his Mount to eye Rorou with vengeance. It opened its mouth and blew a stream of roaring flame. Rorou, caught off guard, didn't dodge but instead constructed a tower shield to hide behind. The flame hit with force. It was more like standing beneath a waterfall than a stream of plasma.

When the holocaust ended, Rorou stood, ready to go on the offensive but the flames stopped him. The ice was burning! *HOW?* he wondered somewhere in the back of his mind. He stared at the flames, watching them dance, intently, as they did the impossible right before his eyes. His warrior instincts screamed at him but he ignored them.

He knew he should move. He was in battle, but the flames...

Shefa watched the three Mounted Riders in the center fall into a flying V formation and bare down on him. He stopped. Stomped, clapped his hands before him hard enough to drown the howl of the wind, and before the force could dissipate, he channeled it into a fist-sized beam that punched the lead Mounted Rider square in the chest. The Rider bowed back so drastically Shefa thought he must have broken its back.

The Mount continued forward. Without pause, Shefa circled his arms in a figure eight motion and turned the monster's forward momentum due left. The creature flew sideways into the charger next to it, taking both down in a tumbling heap, but now the third was on him. Head lowered to skewer, the Rider breathed flame, wings spread, both tails up and poised to strike.

Shefa lept. The flames followed. He spun in midair. The Rider swung. He landed lightly on the Mount's nose, launched off, uppercutting the Rider hard under the chin as he flew past. The stinger tail darted for his heart. He cinched it in both hands as he sailed past and ripped the stinger free in a gout of black blood.

When he landed, his gloves were smoking. The oil that coated the Rider's scales ate at the leather like acid. He shoved his hands in the churned-up snow but it did nothing to ease the poison and the next wave of Mounted Riders was closing fast. He created a field of kinetic energy, expanding it rapidly into a dome, casting the acidic oil off. He watched it running in inky streams down his force field before remembering to check on Rorou.

Rorou was surrounded by flames, hypnotically watching them as if in a trance. Shefa screamed into his mind, *"Roo!"*

The Chimera snapped back with confused fury. He looked around, panicked. He released his conjured shield; it shattered like glass, the shards fading into twinkling silver light before becoming nothing again. The perpetually happy Chimera dropped his head. Lips peeled back from stark white teeth in something in no way related to a smile. Purble energy danced in his eyes. He roared and charged.

The Mount seemed recovered and ready to fight.

Rorou screamed, "Never!" which even he didn't understand.

The Mount snapped its cat-like claws into the ice for traction, then pounced forward into a charge. Rorou dived, came out of his roll and thrust his hands up as if tossing a bowl into the sky. In a flash, he constructed an oblique-edged blade directly beneath the animal. As it rushed forward, it dragged the blade across the underside of its chin, down its throat, through its chest, opening its belly and across the tip of its tail.

The Mount continued on for four bounds more, unraveling its insides with every flex. Stomach, guts and a still-beating heart hit the snow and steamed as the beast fell over dead, never even knowing what killed it. The Mount belted out a cry like a birthing cow; curious sound from such a creature. Rorou constructed a simple staff, shoved it in the mourning creature's mouth then expanded it until he broke the Rider's head apart.

Shefa watched the injured creature stomp and kick in pain and frustration and felt something almost forgotten, excitement. His heart wasn't racing but it had definitely sped up. He felt a smile. He killed it. Before the monster could turn its attention to him, he summoned *LEX*, the magical energy that filled the spaces between all things, and cast a fireball hot enough to warp stone.

It launched with a burst that rocked him back. It slammed into the Mounted Rider like steel, knocking it back as the oil it secreted exploded into hellish bright red flame. The monster bawled, flailing as its flesh melted beneath scales designed to prevent just that.

Four more of the monsters stopped their charge. Across the field, a handful wheeled around to run down his clanmate but saw one of their own dying and halted. Together they watched artificial life experience a painful and very real death. Maybe they had never seen one die before, Shefa thought. Maybe they just hadn't seen one die screaming. Either way, they knew now what they faced.

"Come," the lord of Fuumashon whispered on the wind.

Come they did.

Rorou watched the herd pause in their horror. He could smell the thing dying even in the frozen wind. It smelled of sulfur and the paste that grows between the toes of infected feet. As four of them watched their friend melt into slag, the Chimera constructed a war hook, a curved blade with an opening big enough to saddle a horse, on a polearm twenty feet long. He crept up behind the closest Mounted Rider and swung like a man possessed.

The hook caught the Rider around the waist, just above the joining and below its protective scales. It sliced into the soft tissue below the thing's ribs with a wet sucking sound. He modified his polearm into two curved handles and jerked with supreme violence. The blade ate hungrily. He was halfway through the monster's guts before it knew it was under attack.

He constructed a platform beneath him, with sharp angled ramps to brace his feet against for traction and with angry urgent jerks, he sawed the wailing Rider clear free of its Mount. Liquid tar poured out of the squirming monster as it splatted in the snow. Even as the Rider lay there bleeding out, his companions watched the other burn, unaware that death was creeping up behind them.

He crept up on the next, silent as a shadow under the howling wind,this time holding a spear with a serrated blade. As soon as he got in range, both tails lashed at him. He batted the stinger aside and blocked the club, which knocked him on his back. He expected the Mount to turn about but instead, it charged away from him.

Six great bounds, then it leapt into the sky, beat its massive wings and took flight! Rorou thought the wings were vestigial, ornamental; it never occurred to him that these enormous things could actually fly. The two on the ground turned on him, claws gripping the earth, ready to launch.

Rorou constructed bands around their ankles, as rooted as the stone beneath them. They surged forward, snapping their front paws in a squealing tumble of confused pain. The Mounts brayed at the bones jutting out of their flesh. Burning tears streaked the creatures' faces, too hot to freeze even here. The Riders struggled to upright themselves, pushing futilely against the tons of muscle that landed atop them. Lashing tails struck at nothing in a rage born of desperation. Rorou ran them down.

The first Rider's eyes bulged. Wheezing, struggling, helpless. His Mount pawed at the air, making a wail that wounded the heart. He didn't know for sure but he thought the beast was crying and it touched something soft in him. The Chimera constructed a needle the length of his forearm, thin as the quill of a feather. As the Rider twitched and panted, too afraid to do more, in too much pain to think straight, Rorou slowly poured that blade through the monster's eye.

His breath was hot and sticking, somehow not freezing as it left his mouth. Rorou leaned in. Streaks and wrinkles appeared in the Rider's eye as he twisted forward and back. A wet gurgling let him know he was through the eye and into the brain, so he turned slower.

When the Rider fell back, tension seeping out of its muscles, Rorou released a breath he didn't know he had been holding. As he moved to the second downed Rider, the beast that flew off bore down on him. Rorou was not going to dodge; he was going to murder this stupid bastard.

Head lowered, horns aimed, Rider and Mount descended. Rorou waited, counting the fractions of seconds, his breath drying out his lips. It was too cold to sweat but he needed to. He ached but didn't know why. He set his feet and knees. Relaxed his lower back. He forced himself to blink now so he wouldn't have to later.

Rorou constructed a solid wall of energy. The Mount didn't flinch. The Rider threw up its arms in defense. They plunged through the wall. There was no impact, nothing solid there, only a thin sheet of color to obscure his movement. Massive forepaws hit the snow, digging deep furrows as the mount slid to a stop. The Rider whipped around, searching for its prey.

Rorou landed on the Mount's back and snatched a hook through the Rider's cheek, in one side of its face and clean out the other. Brown blood and pointed teeth shot out the sides of its face. He stood on the Mount's haunches, gripping its stinger like an angry viper. As he bent the Rider backward by the hook piercing its face, he forced its own stinger into its back, just between the shoulder blades with a satisfying click as it shattered scale and chipped into the spine.

The Mount bucked and kicked. Its clubbed tail came in hard. Rorou tilted the Rider to take the blow on the shoulder, snapping it down hard at an ugly angle. The Rider only gasped as wide black eyes stared at the wreath of ribs protruding through its side. Rorou stamped down on the Mount and it responded by pumping all the poison it had deep into its Rider. Rorou watched just long enough to be sure the Rider was too far gone to save then leaped off.

Shefa was pumped. He didn't want to win so much as he wanted to destroy something. He summoned kinetic energy from the earth beneath him, just enough to make him a force of nature. As four Mounted Riders wheeled around to run him down, he steadied himself to get over the feeling that he might physically explode. He waited until they were too close to dodge.

The two in the center opened their mouths, unnatural flames streaming toward him. He interlaced his fingers, pointing both index, creating a crossbow with his hands. He fired a *KINBLAST*, a devastating cone of pure force that swallowed the charge in a rippling distortion and screaming thunder.

KINBLASTS permeated an object, hitting every molecule at almost the exact same moment. The Mounted Riders weren't crushed, they were torn apart cell by cell. Dark grey skin and blood red scales became a wave of pink mist rising on a cloud of fresh steam that was ice a heartbeat ago. The shockwave hit three full seconds before the sound reached the rest of the yard, freezing everyone in their tracks.

The three remaining Mounted Riders who, a moment ago were heart set on ripping Rorou into bite-sized pieces, could only stare in silence at the devastating display of power. While they watched, Rorou constructed twin spears and threw himself at the distracted creatures. He stabbed out left and right, taking both Riders in the neck.

He drew his blades back and stabbed again and again, hard, punching smoking holes in the monsters. The third Rider prepared to charge the distracted Chimera, unaware of the two Northmen positioned behind it, Axis at the ready.

The NUUK and the prince struck as one. The Mounted Rider screamed as both tails came off in two perfect swipes. The Northmen moved forward, a perfect military unit, and struck as one again. They took both wings from the Mount and while it wailed, rushed forward and took both wings from the Rider.

When it finally leaped and wheeled around to face its attackers, Dridden's lunge was already in motion. He caught the Rider in the center of its chest. Bendlin plunged his blade into the Mount's left eye, then quick as doubt, took the right.

"Ho!" the prince shouted as he withdrew his blade.

In the same instant, Bendlin shoved his blade in the same hole, harder and deeper. Then the prince went to work. He slashed away; hand, arm, ear, horn, Rider, Mount, both. He was a blur of bloody violence. Bendlin's blade kept the monster pinned in whining pitiful pain while his former prince literally butchered the helpless creature. Finally, its legs gave out and tipped over. Blood that stank and black as oil, spread across the ice, refusing to freeze, dissolving all it touched.

Dridden was panting from the assault. Bendlin noted his blade was smoking from the acidic secretion from the Rider, but he also noted his blade looked no worse for wear. The glass-steel weapons of this region were designed to kill these beasts. He eyed the Rider harshly, securing eye contact before slowly forcing its chest open with a hissing crack and the smell of sewage. The monster died with a sharp shudder and spurt of blood from each nostril.

"See? Fun, right?" Rorou asked the Northmen who had to smile at his madness.

"Now, let's rip this fucking place to the ground," Shefa said, marching determinedly to the prison's front door.

The others shrugged and followed him, finally considering the possibility of surviving.

THE OLD DIVIDE AND CONQUER

"It's not that I enjoy killing. I just happen to be really good at it."

The front doors were long out of use. The red bricks slurped up whatever light trickled in from the grey sky and swallowed it without remorse. Shefa led the way, his eyes as good in the night as they were at noon. His second set of eyelids amplified even the dimmest light one hundred-fold. The others followed tentatively, especially after Rorou ran off and came back with something that stank like Hell itself.

They traveled through a long hallway. The instant echoes placed both walls close enough to touch. After uncountable time, they emerged into a courtyard too beautiful for where they'd found it.

The open courtyard stretched out for three-hundred paces before them. It was well lit, almost glowing, but the thick grey clouds never let the sun shine bright enough for the way the room lumed. The ever-falling snow melted overhead leaving the space in a churning cloud of fog. It was like waking in a dream. In the center of the courtyard was an altar of some sort, older than even the arrival of the first Northmen.

Seven pillars, one-hundred feet tall, encircled a ring of gold set into the stone, covered in sigils none there could read. A star twenty paces across filled the middle of the golden circle, each point covered in ancient Dwarven script. They didn't know if they were stories or poems or just simple warnings, but they radiated power, old and threatening.

Shefa went to the center of the structure and sat. He crossed his legs before him, closed his eyes and breathed himself into a state of pure calm. The Northmen wandered around, taking in the beauty hidden from all but the worst scum of the earth for hundreds of years.

Each brick had wards of dampening. Each brick was lacquered in some clear finish that wouldn't ever yield to the elements. Each brick carried the love and attention to detail of a master craftsman, and most impressively, no two bricks carried the same hand.

"Must have taken a million dwarves to build this place," Bendlin whispered in reverence.

"What are we waiting for? Let's do what we came to do and leave this place. Every second brings us closer to a screaming death worthy of the bards," Dridden added, his fear making him dramatic.

Rorou walked over to Shefa, calmly, placing each foot carefully and softly before taking the next step. At the edge of the golden circle, he tossed the thing he'd went back out into the cold to collect. Shefa didn't move. He didn't open his eyes. It flew in at his face and froze, frost leaping off in a plume at the sudden stop.

It broke apart and ripped itself into thin strips, hovering three feet off the ground. It tore itself down to equal pieces, solid from liquid, all floating, each piece neatly separated from the whole. Clearly, Shefa was manipulating this. Whatever power he was using wasn't magic. There was no doubt in any of their minds that no magic would work here. The innermost piece moved toward his face. Shefa opened his mouth, eyes still closed and bit down as it floated into his mouth.

"Is that what I think it is?!" Dridden barked.

"It is," Rorou assured him.

Dridden immediately threw up. Rorou swallowed hard to keep from following suit.

Bendlin stepped forward, slowly, squinting in disgusted disbelief. "Is that ... paw?"

"It is. From one of those things out there."

"Why the fuck is he eating it?!"

"That's the source of his power. He's covered in parasites. They take whatever he eats and somehow add it to him, as if they rewrite his blood to include the properties of whatever he shoves in his gullet."

"So, if he ate a bird he could fly?"

"Not exactly. But he might grow wings or at least feathers. The *Pform*, the parasites he's bonded with, don't grant him power; they change his body. If he ate a chameleon, he may develop color-changing skin, but he wouldn't suddenly grow a tail. The parasites improve him to improve their own chances of survival and a tail wouldn't do much good."

"Marvelous creatures. Do you have any?"

"Fuck the gods, no! They also change your mind. Most become mad beasts. He's the only one ever known to *somewhat* keep his wits. And you see how sane he is. They're quite the scourge back home. You should visit some time."

"Thank you, no. Our deal was: take him to the Kalmar and he would take me someplace warm."

"Fuumashon is warm," Rorou said with a laugh that made Bendlin think he was almost certainly going to the land of brain slugs and dragon men. A shiver ran up his spine that had nothing to do with the cold.

There were seven doors leading off the main keep. Each one looked equally evil. Wood the color of lilac, bound in iron painted red with heavy locks, reminded them this was a prison and not a church. Bendlin took long, deep breaths to calm his mind. Dridden paced. Rorou watched Shefa. Shefa sniffed the air. After sniffing and turning to each door in turn, Shefa pointed to one.

"That's the winner?" Rorou asked.

"It stinks worse than the rest. Got everything you need?"

Rorou flashed him a look that said, "Don't insult me."

"Meet in the middle?"

"Race you."

"No. Promised to return them, 'member?"

"Ah. Shame."

"No worries. Plenty of fun to be had."

"Oooh. The unknown?"

"Better. Whatever lives through that door is not from this plane," Shefa explained.

Rorou nearly salivated at the thought. "Demons?"

"For you, my friend, here's hoping."

Shefa extended his hand. Rorou took him by the forearm. They pulled each other close with a half hug and kissed foreheads, the soldier's farewell.

"Until all are one," they said in unison and let go.

They looked each other in the eye, sharing a look that friends who fear they will never meet again try to hide, but these men embraced it. They were brave but they weren't stupid. They didn't behave the way they did because they didn't think they could die; exactly the opposite. They behaved the way they did because they expected to die. It was freeing. It was their way of raging against the inevitable and refusing to let fear dictate their actions. It was the response of young men too inexperienced to realize old is better than dead.

"Prince. Let's go."

Shefa headed back out into the snow.

"Where are we going?" Dridden asked as he followed Shefa, worried and angry.

Rorou looked to Bendlin and smiled. "I know I come off as some sort of lunatic, but you have my word that by my life or my death, if I can keep you alive, I shall."

Bendlin snorted. "I trust him. I don't trust you."

"I *don't* trust him and I *do* trust you. So, we should be fine. Now let's go see if we can rustle up a demon or two to slay."

Rorou started off with a spring in his step, his long black hair bouncing off his shoulders. Bendlin blew out a long sigh and wondered,

not for the last time that day, what gods-damned horrible way he was
going to die.

Shefa and Dridden stood in the snow, staring up at the top of
the tower.

"What are we looking at?"

"That window. It's open."

"What window?"

"Your human eyes can't see it, but I can."

"I'm impressed," the northern prince said dryly. "Why are
we—wait, *you*—looking at that window?"

"Because that's our way in."

Before the prince could panic, Shefa grabbed the man and his
weapons, cast *levitate* and fired a *KINBLAST* straight down. They shot
up like a cork, Dridden screaming his head off the whole way. The
flight was longer than a breath, so he screamed himself dry, inhaled,
and screamed some more.

They landed rougher than Shefa expected but certainly softer than
Dridden expected. Shefa set the man down, patted him on the head
and left him to his panic attack.

Shefa stared down the red hall. It was as if the walls were flashing
him an evil grin. Death lived here and she was not a pleasant host. He
tried to discern if it was his fear or some warrior instinct warning him.

He was Chimera, a warrior crafted from earth and glass for exactly
this, but he carried all the emotions of the primary races. He wasn't
fearless; he was just very good at controlling his fear. This place was
testing his resolve. Dridden stood next to him, wiping the last of the
freezing vomit from his lips.

"Man wasn't meant to fly," he said, voice shaky.

Shefa ignored him. "What do you know about this place?"

Dridden sighed. "Tower One, RavenHold. Seven floors. Officer's quarters are on level three. Primarily for lesser offenders. Conquerors, torturers, tyrants. Human scum."

"What else?"

Dridden looked at Shefa closely. A dawning realization hit that there might be a person behind that stone-cold facade. "Is that fear I hear in your voice?"

Without pause, Shefa said, "Yes."

Dridden wanted to laugh. He wanted to mock the stranger from the south but he couldn't. He had seen Shefa's power. Whatever had him scared was truly to be feared. Shefa blew out a long, calming breath and started walking.

The hall was long and quiet. Frigid air from outside mixed with the meager warmth trapped inside the tower, making the air moist and moldy. The walls were slick with moisture, giving them a sick feverish appearance. Light from the window lit the passage well enough, though Dridden kept his head leaping from shadow to shadow.

There were no cobwebs here. There were no carcasses of tiny animals, not even rat scat. A few patches of frost coated the bricks but did nothing to diminish their craftsmanship. He thought perhaps the cold kept the smarter creatures deeper in the tower, but still, something nagged at him. The hall ended at a corner that opened into a massive room that spanned the whole width of the tower. Cells covered every inch of the room's perimeter, thirty-two in all.

Shefa clapped once, hard. Sharp as a crack of thunder, it filled the room bouncing hard off the stone walls. What appeared to be corpses stirred. Gaunt, haunting, emaciated faces peeled off the cold floor to focus hollow eyes on him. A few reached out toward him. Most were too weak and simply watched.

"This is not justice," Shefa growled to the prince. "If their crimes warrant it, kill them and be done with it, but this is cruel and serves no purpose." He headed over to the nearest cell.

"They're criminals. They *earned* their fate," Dridden explained as though Shefa simply didn't understand.

Shefa threw daggers with his eyes then turned to the wilted man in the cell. "What is your name?"

"C-cold," the man stuttered.

Shefa summoned a handful of flame to warm the man but the spell didn't work; he couldn't reach the *LEX*.

"No magic here, remember?" Dridden spit at him.

Shefa eyed the man again, more dangerously this time. He ripped a bar out of the cell wall and used it to stab away at the bricks until he revealed a wooden support beam buried within, then tore the beam from the wall and carried it to the middle of the room. He kneeled and fell into himself. This time he didn't step into the hall between matter and energy, searching for cosmic energy to contort. He found the latent potential energy that existed within the wood and agitated it ten times over.

The surface of the beam began to smoke. He had to focus the *KIN*; he didn't want an explosion, he just wanted enough friction to start a fire. After a minute or so, the surface of the beam caught light. He sagged in relief. Making things blow up came easily; this level of control was exhausting.

As the wood creaked and popped, belching smoke and shedding marginal heat, Shefa started opening all the cells.

"What are you doing, southern fool?" the prince asked through bared teeth, hefting his Axis.

Shefa turned and marched over to the man. He stopped a finger's length from his nose. He said nothing. He did nothing. Dridden stared down at the Chimera, his breath coming quick and sharp, his eyes leaping left to right, hoping to find some clue to the southerner's intention. Shefa was a blank slate.

"I promised your father," he said.

No one moved. No one spoke.

Dridden calmed. "Yes, you did." A small smirk tugged at the corner of his mouth. The fool had wisened.

"My promise is kept the moment you step foot back in that room," Shefa reminded him.

The smirk died on his face. Shefa went back to prying open the cages. He helped starving men and two women to the middle of the room where they could feel the heat. One woman, small, hair that was probably blonde once but too dirty to know for sure now, waved him over.

He kneeled before her. "What can I—"

She jabbed a sharp piece of stone into his throat, her eyes wild with hate. The frozen flint snapped against his scale-hard skin. He didn't even flinch. She went into a fit, swatting at him with what feeble strength remained in her desiccated body.

"You see?! Human scum! You can't treat these people like human beings, they're animals with—"

A small man had crawled over and bounced her head off the floor, leaving a crack in her brittle forehead. Shefa grabbed her by the ankle and hoisted her off the ground. He laid her gently on the burning beam and used her body to stoke the flames. She did what little screaming she could as he slid her back and forth across the open flame like a frying pan. None of the other prisoners seemed bothered by the act.

Dridden stared wide-eyed at the callousness. This man just went out of his way to save her and just as casually cooked her alive. This is was a true monster. Once the rags she wore as clothes caught, he let her go and watched her pathetic attempt to crawl off the fire. She didn't get far. Without a word, Shefa left the room.

The other door led to the stairs which spiraled down to the next level. Shefa wandered in stoic silence. Piles of frozen bodies littered the floor, a thin layer of ice sealing them to it. This room was warmer than the one above, but with no way to escape the wet floor, the prisoners here could never get warm. He stopped, clenching his fists in muted rage.

"You saw what happened when you showed these people kindness. That bitch tried to tear your throat out." Dridden's words were almost conciliatory.

Shefa's were verklempt. "One tried to kill me. One tried to save me. Because they're people. Individuals. Separate and unique. You lump them all into this category or that and believe you know them. You don't know them. They are not cows or Bleeders or whatever shitty stupid beasts you have in this frozen shithole. They think, they feel, and above all, they change ... because they're *people*, you ignorant fuck." Shefa left the floor.

Dridden caught up to Shefa on the stairs. "Why do you care?"

"About what?"

"Scum. You came here barking orders, hurting good folk, and now you want to shed frozen tears for a pack of mongrels that should have been executed on the spot. I would say you're feeling guilty but I'm not sure you can. So?"

Shefa turned around and faced the man. He already stood head and shoulders above the Chimera. Standing two steps behind, Shefa was nearly staring straight up.

"What is the point?" Shefa asked. Dridden looked confused. "Prison. What's the point?"

"Is this a joke? Some kind of riddle?"

"Gods, you're dumb. No, it's not a joke or riddle. Why did people invent jails?"

"To keep order. To let the people know certain behavior wouldn't be tolerated."

"So, to scare the peasants into proper behavior?"

"No! That's what mam's and da's are for. Jail is for those who don't heed the law. Lessons must be taught. Order must be maintained."

"So, jail is a punishment for bad decisions?"

"I know you have a point you want to make, so just make it already."

"If the point of prison is punishment, then it serves no point at all. You take bad people and lock them up with worse people, what do you think you get in the end? If you're not gonna correct their thinking, teach them the lessons they obviously missed or they wouldn't be there in the first place, how will they ever function outside of these walls? Punishment isn't rehabilitation and if you aren't gonna rehabilitate them, why not just kill 'em outright and be done with it? This is a half-measure that basically amounts to torture."

Shefa didn't move. He wasn't shaking, his eyes weren't rimmed with tears too thin to fall, but a pain rolled off him that even simple Dridden couldn't ignore. It was as if an illusion was standing before him and the true Chimera was weeping beneath it. He couldn't see any outrage, but he could feel it like a hand on his throat.

"C'mon."

All light faded as they neared the bottom of the spiraling stairs. Beyond was an old darkness, the kind that lurks in caves deep underground and hates the light with a palpable fury.

"Stop!" Shefa said, as close to panic as the Northman had ever heard him.

"What?! What's out there?!"

"I don't know ... but it hates us."

Shefa slowly raised his foot, waist high and stomped with a boom. He trapped the energy before it could dissipate and fired a *KINBLAST* into the dark. It sounded like a dying bird falling from the sky. He heard the walls rattle as the force ground past them. He could smell the dirt and dust raining from the ceiling but nothing died. Nothing cried out in pain. But the hairs on his neck still stood straight as a priest.

"Maybe we should run," Dridden offered.

"Run through a room we've never seen while something waits in the dark to ambush us? Doesn't sound like the smartest idea."

Shefa couldn't see it, but Dridden frowned at him. Shefa could usually see in low light environments, not total darkness, but unless he was underground, there was usually *some* light. He could only see black before him. Normally he would assume this was a *darkness* spell but magic wouldn't work here. He didn't like this one bit. He felt something slide past him.

"Did you feel that?"

"Feel what?!"

"Stop yelling, you moron. You give away our position." Shefa scanned the way behind them. It was now darker than the way forward. "Hoist that spear and charge ... now!"

Dridden took off running. He was screaming like he'd fallen off a cliff, poking out in front of him every couple of feet, hoping against reason that whatever was hunting them would be stupid enough to jump in front of his blade. Shefa was right on his heels. They could see a small speck of light in the distance. Without scenery, it was impossible to judge how far away. Dridden cursed and went down in a tumble.

"What happened?!"

"My leg! Something bit me!"

Shefa sniffed the air and found blood, deep blood. This was no nip from a house pet. Something tried to eat him. Shefa moved in, feeling for the prince. He found him and scooped him up.

"You have your Axis?"

"Yes, but I lost my shield," Dridden managed through a pained grunt.

Shefa started moving. The prince wasn't heavy, but he was awkward and difficult to transport. The whining, bleeding, and wiggling didn't help much either. He couldn't see the ground; he had no idea if the next step would drop him in a hole and shatter his ankle or a step that would spill them both, making them easy prey from the monsters hunting them. Still, he ran on.

A sharp pain raked across Shefa's face and neck. He dropped to one knee, refusing to drop the prince, and slid on his kneecap across the uneven stone. He could feel the skin strip away with a spike of throbbing pain.

"Got you, too?!"

"Yeah! But I can't find it! I don't smell it, I can't sense its thoughts. What the hell *is* this thing?!"

Then a warped animal laughter crawled out of the dark. Shefa froze. Every human instinct him told him not to look, never look! He looked. A pair of poppy red eyes slid open in the darkness. They blinked and shifted left to right, then laughed again. Below them and to the left, a second pair of eyes slithered open. Then six more. Then thirty. Then so many eyes it made no sense to count.

"No ... it can't be..." Dridden exhaled in a tone of pure dread.

"Explain, quickly!"

"Nightmares!"

"Nightmares?! Something useful!"

"Stories we tell children! Shadows that come to life to eat the wicked!"

"How do I kill them?!"

"They're Nightmares! You don't kill them, you run!"

Shefa hoisted the prince and bolted. His stride was replaced by an awkward wobbling hobble as the pain in his leg grew too great to be ignored. His neck was bleeding freely and he started to feel light-headed. Dridden watched as the glowing horde of eyes started bounding after them, laughing and keeling like drunks on a ship at sea. Now they could hear the paws slapping the ground, claws raking the stone and husky labored breathing as the monsters ran them down.

Dridden kept repeating, "We're gonna die, we're gonna die," over and over again and it was driving Shefa crazy.

A howl pierced the dark, and a rip opened on Shefa's leg. He went down in a sprawl, careful to keep his body between the prince and the ground. He couldn't see his leg but he could feel the chunk of his calf flapping against his ankle.

"Hahahahaha! Rorou is gonna be so pissed!" Shefa screamed like a madman.

Dridden, by this point, had gone catatonic and stiff as a board. Shefa was close enough to the light to guess the distance. He figured it was also close enough to throw the prince without killing him, barring him landing on his head. Shefa pushed his body up to standing.

The horde was right on top of him. A bark and a bright line of pain shot down his arm. The smell of blood was everywhere, so thick in the air he could taste it. He hoisted the prince by his backplate and his belt and chucked him like raw lumber.

He watched as the prince flew like a spear to the door of light thirty paces away. Three more slashes sliced across his face and scalp, the last almost taking his eye. He covered his head, watched and waited. The sound of slapping feet filled the room; he couldn't tell where they were any more, only that they were too close.

Something struck him like a horse. He felt something rip in his back as he went down, hard. Whatever hit him landed atop him, squeezing the wind out of him. He never took his eyes off the prince. Just before the prince hit the ground, Shefa fired a *KINWAVE*, a rolling carpet of force that broke the prince's fall and slid him safely out into the light.

"YES!" Shefa celebrated.

He was surrounded now. Death was imminent. Something laid a massive paw on his chest, like a cat keeping a mouse in play for later. Shefa tapped the stored energy in his armor, the stored energy in every

Kinstone in his ring, and fired a beam of devastating force to his left. If memory served, that would be the closet wall to outside. The beam exploded against the wall with a deafening roar.

Teeth rattled in Shefa's head, his heart stuttered in his chest as the pressure hit him. Sound was replaced by a long, piercing wail. The stone detonated outward, creating a storm of lethal shrapnel that shattered the outer wall beyond it. The overpressure smashed the dust against the far wall just for a moment before the outward expanding wall created a vacuum effect and sucked it all outside. His nose and mouth filled too quickly to avoid.

Light poured into the room and struck the monsters like fire!

Shefa opened his eyes in time to see a few of the monsters sucked out into the sunlight and an unsurvivable drop, howling the whole way. These monsters were like nothing he had ever seen. They were shadows, truly. Flat as a page from a book.

They resembled iguana the size of hunting dogs. They screeched at the light, terrified, and it ate at them like acid. Shefa fell into that place of perfect hate, of pure selfish rage and murdered every other sensation in his being.

He crawled on hands and knees, punching with roaring force, knocking whimpering shadows out into the sky. They howled, they screamed, they died confused and afraid and Shefa felt no sympathy. The last two, clever beasts hunkered down in a corner, growling and hissing at the crawling food-who-would-not-die. He pushed off with his arms, landing on the monsters, slicing into his bicepson impact. He wrapped his arms around their necks and dragged them into the light.

Deep grooves in ancient stone followed their bodies as they did all they could to stay alive. They didn't even think to bite or scratch him; their fear of the sun was supreme. He held them while they kicked and screeched and screamed and died, shadows melting into pools of rancid oil in his arms. What passed for blood leaked out of them with the smell of molding bread. When they were dead, he dropped his head and blacked out.

Shefa woke up with a start. He quickly oriented himself and all the pain in his body screamed at him. He was sitting in a pool of his own blood mixed with what remained of the Nightmares. He was starving. The *Pform* that gave him the incredible ability to perpetually evolve into more perfect versions of himself also required constant fuel. He ate nearly half as often as he breathed.

The shadows were bubbling pools of oil. There was nothing left of them to eat. He closed his eyes and steadied himself, regulating his breathing and emptying his mind. Before he could reconsider the thought, he rolled over and slurped as much of his blood as he could off the floor, wincing as it touched his lips. It had cooled into more of a gel than a liquid.

The second it hit his throat, salty and almost chewy, he clenched and his stomach retched, trying to force it back out. It smelled like blood but also like oil already used to cook bad meat. Every hair in his nose curled away and his tongue trembled in resistance.

The *Pform* bonded to his body knew the wound was infected and this puddle was poison. Three times the creatures almost forced him to throw up; only his training pushed him through the nausea. When he could take no more, he rolled on his back and used force-breathing techniques to keep the disgusting meal down.

Finally sure he wasn't going to puke, he dug in the small pack he kept at the small of his back and fished out his emergency kit: a roll of meat, a slice of cheese baked into a salted knot of bread, and a small vile of Hundred-berry wine, the Elvin healing elixir. He sipped half the tiny vile and ate desperately. When he was done, he started crawling for the prince.

He the prince was only a short distance away, but crawling on his belly on freezing stone, dragging legs that didn't work; he might as well had been trying to top a mountain. Shefa felt the healing potion start to work. He grabbed the hanging flap of meat and pressed it back in place on his leg. He felt the skin stretch and latch on to severed meat. When the piece was once more a part of him, he let go and continued to crawl.

He made it to the prince who appeared to be sleeping. His leg was opened from knee to ankle; the cut went through his pant and boot like nothing. Shefa was fairly sure his body had destroyed the poison by then and squeezed a few drops of blood from his leg wound into the healing potion. He carefully dripped it into the prince's mouth, waited and hoped. His leg had finally healed enough for him to focus.

He could call on his *LEX*, summon Arcane energy to speed up his healing ... anywhere but here. He cursed himself for forgetting about the dampening stones. He was starting to realize how often he relied on magic, something he would have to change in the future.

It wasn't long before the prince started showing signs of life. The purple skin around the cut on his leg began to ooze black oil before fading back to his normal skin tone. His breathing struggled, face contorting in pain as three weeks' worth of healing took place in as many minutes. The Northman held his breath for several heartbeats then slumped mightily as he released it.

Shefa had seen this process many times before. He always worried one of these times, the potion would finish the job the wound started, but so far it always worked. What was new; in a smooth wave, what passed for red hair, that horrible orange tint, turned to true red, blood red, before his eyes. He knew his blood would have an effect on human physiology but the *Pform* had changed him so much he couldn't be sure what mutations would take root in the prince.

Dridden opened his eyes wide. He sat straight up as though yanked by a rope. He wasn't just awake, he was more alert than he had ever been in his life. He twisted his head left and right, popping the bones in his neck and flexing as though his muscles had a power he had never found in them before. He looked at Shefa, the healing cuts on his face, the close call that could've left him blind, and smirked.

"Did we win?" Dridden asked.

Shefa smirked back. "Let's get the hell off this floor."

"First smart thing you've said since I met you."

They were standing in a vestibule prettier than what they had seen thus far, more ornate. The floor was tiled, mosaic patterns that seemed blue and white from a distance. Up close, each tile was a rainbow of colors that together formed a new and unique whole. Each tile must have taken tens of hours of labor. The ceiling was double high and no runes covered the bricks.

They moved toward the stairs, Dridden at an enthusiastic pace, Shefa still nursing his wounds. As they rounded the stairs, Dridden noticed Shefa was falling behind and slowed to check on him.

"That little scratch causing you trouble?"

"I gave my healing potion to you."

Dridden wanted to say something glib but found he didn't have it in him. He offered Shefa a shoulder; Shefa stared for a moment, trying to recognize the gesture then burst into laughter. Dridden scowled, thinking he was being mocked somehow but the laughing went on so long he soon found himself giggling without knowing why.

"What are we laughing about?"

"That was very ... sweet of you. Thank you," he said with a chuckle. "The parasites bonded to me require a lot of energy. I'm almost always hungry. I'm not sick or injured, I'm just exhausted. Once I eat, I'll be better."

Dridden felt something strange. He wanted to call it sympathy but there was no way he was feeling sorry for this walking massacre. But seeing him struggle made him more likable somehow.

He was covered in filth from head to toe. Black oil and dried blood stained his face and arms; the cuts still had a lot of healing to do and his leg looked septic. His hair looked like he had spent a week on horseback in howling storms.

Dridden went into his boot and pulled out a sleeve of sweaty meat. It was leaking blood and covered in leg hair, but the prince offered it in thanks. Shefa wanted to be disgusted but he still had blood he'd slurped off the floor drying on his face.

"Hold on to it. If you don't need it, I'll take it. I'm fine for now."

"You look like Hell."

"You look like a new man. Did you get taller?"

"Don't know. Funny, I feel sixteen again!"

"I gave you my blood."

"I drank your blood?" he asked horrified, face curled into the love-child of disgust and anger.

"Worked, didn't it?"

"Well, yeah, I guess. I feel brand new."

"I feel like shit. Weak, hobbled … human. Let's get this over with."

They winded down the stairs, dozens of them, each bend bringing them closer to a rising din. Below was filled with the sound of many voices; not happy ones. As they spiraled down, it became concerning. There was no metal on metal, so it didn't sound like a battle; it sounded more like a riot. A few minutes later, they finally reached the fourth floor.

The stairs opened into a round open room, obviously designed as refuge for the officers assigned to this armpit. Six pillars divided the room into three long aisles. A massive table dominated the middle of the room, and couches, lounges and floor pillows lined the walls with a single hall at the far end crammed full of rowdy bodies.

The floors were more of those beautiful mosaic tiles. Here, they started blue at one door and gradually faded to yellow at the far end. There were no paintings or tapestries, but the walls were smooth, glazed and polished in a style neither of the intruders had ever seen in their travels.

"What do you figure they're so upset about?"

"No doubt in my mind. That many people, that mad? It *has* to be Rorou."

The men were all dressed in poor leather armor, the kind brigands pieced together from their victims. The carried a variety of weapons; swords, clubs, canes, bows—everything one would need to take a small town by storm.

"If you wanna sit this one out…" Dridden said, stepping forward.

"There's probably fifty of them over there."

Dridden started to say something smooth, the kind of line a hero would throw back in a grand story told around a drinking hall, but Dridden wasn't a smart man.

Shefa decided to help him out. "Those poor bastards."

Dridden nodded his thanks and twirled his Axis. His whistle cut like glass. Every other sound in the room stopped at the sheer volume of the sound. All eyes were on him.

"I am Dridden, son of Grond, leader of the High Guard at AlinHall and prince of the Whitelands. Kneel before your prince." No one moved. Dridden smiled like the devil. "Treason!" he roared as he charged the mob.

They roared back and rushed to meet him. Shefa smiled darkly. There were a whole lot of bodies moving. This would be fun.

Shefa began to siphon. Every flexing muscle. Every pounding foot. Every heaving chest, screaming throat, and rattling saber. Dridden was bigger than the largest bandit by half a head. When they collided, he was going to plow himself into the center of the mob and die like a true Northman. Shefa would've been proud of the fool if he didn't have a promise to keep.

He interlaced his fingers, steepling the pointers, and fired. Enough force to stop a charging man cold was squeezed into a beam thinner than a finger. The man leading the charge felt a sharp pain in his chest then found his arms didn't work. Dridden sliced the man from collar to crotch and bowled him and the three behind him clean over.

Blades came at him from every angle, but he knew no fear. The prince of the Whitelands swung like a man convinced he was a god. He knocked three men back with a mighty roar and slashed one across the throat while slicing another across the thigh. Blood sprayed around him in a beautiful wave. He punched out with that bladed handguard and sunk it to the hilt in some poor bastard's face, just below the eyes. The man's eyes danced spastically as his nose peeled from his face.

Before Dridden could pull the blade free, the man's head exploded. Brain splattered across the prince's face, making him flinch in surprise. Dridden cut his eyes over and saw Shefa standing there, arm extended, pointer finger quivering, thumb up and angry. The Chimera flashed him a wink and the big man committed a massacre. It was fun. It was a practice session. It was a consequence-free expression of all the hate a petulant child had accumulated over a lifetime.

He slashed at eyes and ears, savoring the screams as men fell away dying. Block, parry, stab, then watch a pile of bodies crumple. He was drunk. He was high. He was riding lightning with an angel on his shoulder making sure no blade ever found him. He spun his blade over one hand, under the other then around and behind his back, the whole time watching as holes appeared in his foes with a wet punch and a pained "oof."

Dridden stabbed a man in the chest so hard the blade struck his spine. The man grunted, cinched and blew his out bowels. Bodies started piling up, grabbing at his heels, swatting at his feet. The floor was growing slick with body fluids. With a bawl, the giant red head from the north raised his boot and stomped a man's head, cracking the skull and dislodging an eye. Then another. Then one more.

Shefa moved closer, worried about missing his target and leaving the prince open. He was using both hands now, firing left and right as fast as he could pick a target. They weren't all kill shots. Some he just fired into a group of bodies and watched the fallout. He shot at every swinging blade, swinging fist, screaming mouth, kicking boot—if it wasn't Dridden, he shot it.

As the men came to realize there were more of them lying than standing, they started to break and run. Shefa shot them down, easy picking for the prince to finish off. Dridden ran a few down, sticking men hard between the shoulder blades before ripping the blade up in a shower of gore.

Shefa hobbled over to the door the mob was beating against when they arrived. It was an ironbound door in an iron frame; a fall-back room in case the inmates took the tower. He knocked on the door; once, twice, twice again, then once.

"Had enough fun yet?"

He waited.

Dridden was finishing off those foolish enough to draw his attention by crawling rather than playing dead. A series of locks clicked, clacked, and something slid into the wall. A moment later, the door began to slowly creak open.

"No such thing," Rorou said.

The door screeched open, revealing a sight like no other. Blood was everywhere. There were no bodies, just chunks of meat, bits of bone and lots and lots of blood. Rorou sat at a desk that was large and regal and may have been beautiful under all that sick, with his feet up smoking something whose scent was lost in the stench of dead flesh. Bendlin was emptying his guts on a bookshelf against the back wall. Dridden stepped in slowly, eyes wide, scanning the stains on the floor, walls, and ceiling.

"What ... happened in here?" the prince asked in a broken whisper.

"A good time was had by all," Rorou said, then blew a smoke ring and sniffed it back up his nose before it floated away. Dridden turned to empty his guts out in the main room but didn't have the fuel. The dry heaving sounded horrendous.

Shefa shook his head. "Must you always?"

"Must I? No," the cocky Chimera said with a look halfway between a threat and a smile. "Looks like you were wrong; no demons."

"Who do you think did this?" Shefa said, indicating his bruises. Jealous anger flared in Rorou's beautiful brown eyes. "I need to eat," Shefa said.

Both Northmen began heaving anew.

7

FUN, FUN, FUN

"I love him as a brother. I hate him as only a brother could."

S hefa watched Rorou and Bendlin head west on a bridge of purble light. They moved with the easy confidence of men off to go fishing. That wasn't unusual, Rorou had always moved with easy confidence. Bendlin was simply so loyal that he moved as required to serve. He was an exceptional man. Shefa hadn't said that about many humans.

"Will this tower be as fun as the last?" Bendlin asked Rorou as they stepped off the bridge at the base of the lower west tower.

"One can only hope."

There was a knotted rope hanging from the lowest widow just above a door, barricaded for permanent disuse. Clearly it was there to circumvent the defunct doors but Rorou had another idea. He constructed a war spike, a four-foot conical hammerhead on a twelve-foot staff. He swung it with a deep chested grunt, shattering the door with a ruckus no one inside could ignore.

"Do you *want* them to know we're coming?" Bendlin scolded. Rorou eyed him dangerously, a touch of squint, a touch of madness. "Of course you do," he said with a resigned sigh.

They climbed past the debris into the dark. There were no lights on the bottom floor; only what came in through the door lit the room. As they crunched over shattered doors and frozen stone, Bendlin could swear he recognized a particular sound; a dry, resistant *crick* as something snapped underfoot. His eyes were not what they used to be; even with the Cyan ring, the poor lighting didn't help. He leaned forward, inspecting the floor before him.

"Bones," Rorou said. "Thousands and thousands of bones. Decades old. Not just animal. Human, too."

"Human ... bones? This many?"

"Yes, Bennie. We have stumbled upon a nest of cannibals."

Bendlin couldn't see him but he could hear the smile in his voice. Bendlin followed the Chimera's footsteps to the stairs and together they climbed. Three revolutions brought them to a well-lit floor decorated more like a training dojo than a prison ward. A single yellow crystal fixed to the ceiling threw strange pulsing light into a series of mirrors that seemed to light the entire room evenly.

The floor was covered with sand that couldn't have come from anywhere within a hundred miles, used to break falls, Rorou assumed. Swords, pikes, glaives, and staffs hung on crude hooks fastened to the walls and of course, those walls were exposed red brick. The room smelled of sweaty ass, infected feet, and just a hint of crushed lavender, as if someone tried to freshen a corpse with a bouquet. It was retched.

"What do you see?" Bendlin asked, adjusting his grip on his Axis.

Rorou closed his eyes. Behind his lids a faint light reddened the pink of his flesh, letting Bendlin know he was using his *ALL SIGHT.* Since birth, Rorou was able to look at the world with spiritual eyes. It was as if his soul left his body and gained access to powers beyond the capabilities of flesh. In short, he could "see" almost anything he wanted if he only knew how to look for it. He was looking for anger, confusion, and rage.

"We are not alone," the Chimera said when he came back.

"How many?"

"Too many."

"TOO many?!"

"Yes."

Rorou scanned the room, a nervous energy about him. He looked at Bendlin with sympathetic eyes, almost as if he had already seen the man's death. He cut his eyes away and looked at Bendlin again, but this time he smiled, all emotion snuffed out.

"I may die, but *you* have to make it back. I promised Shefa and one does not break a promise to that madman!"

Bendlin blanched at that. Rorou was calling someone a madman? What sort of monster must Shefa turn into?!

"Well, if you die, his thoughts on the matter won't really matter," Bendlin said with dark humor.

Rorou shook his head. "You don't know him at all. Stay back. Wait until we see what their gimmick is and above all else, even your life, DO WHAT I SAY WHEN I SAY IT!"

He stared at him with an intensity that made his face itch. Bendlin nodded sharply.

Rorou walked to the center of the room. He snapped his fingers. Three seconds later, he did it again. And so it went, every three seconds he snapped. It may have been a minute; it may have been a week, hard to tell in the moments before battle. The crystal illuminating the room doubled its brightness then winked out completely. They were suddenly blind and an unnatural panic set in. The light came back a heartbeat later while Rorou was still shaking the flash image from his mind.

He was surrounded by twenty men; thin, hard, dressed in black from head to toe. Only a slit in their masks showed their eyes. They stood in perfect formation. One every three degrees, encircling him, eight inches between them. These were professional assassins, *true* blood workers. Rorou felt a bead of sweat run between his shoulder blades; his mouth started to water.

The light snapped off. Blackness encroached like death. He could hear movement, breathing, he could feel the disturbance in the air as they shifted around the room. He was tense. Excited. A shiver ran up his spine. This could be it, he thought, the moment he left the limitations and the burden of his body behind. It was exhilarating.

The light pushed out the dark in a mad rush. It stung the eyes, not that it mattered; he was alone again. Laughter burst out of Rorou, loud pure raucous amusement and the handsome Chimera applauded their talent. Clearly, the move was meant to intimidate, but Rorou couldn't help but appreciate the dedication required, not to mention the rehearsal, to master such an elegant maneuver.

"Magnificent! Your troupe is the best I've ever seen and I have seen more than most. Who is in charge, that I may congratulate you properly?"

Nothing happened for several seconds. The light fell away. Rorou constructed a tower beneath him, lifting him ten feet into the air. He counted the seconds and released the construct just in time to be standing in his original spot as the light came on. Light returned and a man stood before him, dressed in black, mask removed.

He was old, too old to be fighting let alone at this level of fitness. His eyes were milky grey with age but blue once, he thought. He had a strange, almost perfectly circular scar in the middle of his face, cresting his nose, cutting across both eyes and his upper lip as if someone tried to shove a pipe through his face. Salt and pepper hair clung to his scalp in defiance of time and a small chunk of his left ear was missing.

"I am Crayton. My men are the best in the Whitelands and at least three hundred leagues beyond. What is the obstacle you would like removed?"

The man's voice was right out of a storybook; gruff and deep, demanding respect and promising suffering.

Rorou cocked an eyebrow in response. "You were expecting me," he said in a tone halfway between a statement and a question.

"Not exactly, but it doesn't take the son of Krastis to figure that a man who comes to DragonHold is in need of blood work," the old man said with a crooked grin, the left side of his face unresponsive.

The southerner had no idea who or what Krastis was and even less of a clue about his son, but he got the message.

"Your troupe is magnificent, truly! Unfortunately, there has been a misunderstanding. I have not come to hire you." Crayton stiffened, almost too subtly to notice but Rorou missed very little. "I have been sent to test you."

"You sound like a fool. What is it you want?" the assassin asked, annoyed.

"My employer does need some work done. Normally I handle his affairs, but this requires multiple bodies, and before I trust my back to someone, I like to know that they are competent," Rorou lied with expert liquidity. He loved stories and found telling them came as easy as breathing.

"I can prepare a demonstration," Crayton said.

Rorou opened his mouth to speak, then paused and looked up. It was time for the light to go out. It didn't.

"Oh, very clever," Rorou said, impressed. He didn't know how they controlled the light, but he would figure it out later since he had already decided he was taking it with him when he left. "Just bring out the men and step back. I'll inspect them myself."

Crayton stepped back and a series of trap doors opened in the floor, walls, and ceilings. They were all tiny things that no man should have been able to fit into. Blood workers slithered out like boneless predators. A heartbeat later, they were formed up for inspection.

"Crayon, was it?"

"CrayTON."

"Yes. Are there any in your employment who are not combatants?"

"You mean like a maid? No."

"Oh, splendid! No worries about severance pay then."

A purble mist rushed out from Rorou's feet like a storm cloud. Without warning, a wall of spikes shot out from the mist, impaling the front row. Men grunted and groaned as pikes as thick as a man's wrist punched into their guts and chests with wet *oomphs* and sickening cracks.

Crayton jumped back. The remaining blood workers exploded into action. The light died. After-images made it hard to concentrate. Rorou heard Bendlin grunting and realized that the fool had joined the fight.

"Duck right!"

Rorou summoned a series of spikes from the left wall. They rushed out at armor-piercing speed. He heard the sucking sound that accompanies impaling a man, loud as their screams and gurgles as men died or wished they had. The light pulsed, once. Rorou got a vision of dead bodies frozen in time and space, dead or dying, unable to fall, shackled in that moment.

Sprays of blood seemed more solid than liquid. A detached eye flying in a twirling arch, a spiral of blood leading back to the shattered socket, made his throat tight for a second. One man must have been moving at an impressive speed and caught by multiple spits because he was literally tearing himself into strips as he dashed with holy horror in his wide, bloodshot eyes.

Darkness.

"Duck!"

Rorou thrust spikes down from the ceiling. Unfortunately, Bendlin wasn't the only one who dropped. Blood workers were seen as mindless brutes but one didn't survive in such a deadly profession without brains. The light came back and everyone still able leaped up off the floor, charging and drawing weapons he hadn't noticed on them before. Short sickle swords, bladed on both sides hammered out of black metal danced in the yellow light, made lava-orange by the red walls.

Rorou turned toward Bendlin, thirty feet away, too far away to help and screamed in a fragile, broken voice, "MOVING IS FUN!"

The light went out. Rorou dropped to his knees. Bendlin froze. That message made no sense. The fear in his voice made no sense. The fool wasn't afraid to die; he WANTED to die. So what was he trying to say? Then Bendlin felt his body moving. A strange sensation churned in his stomach as he realized he was being lifted into the air.

"Freeze!" he realized.

Butchering was fun for this psychopath; if moving was fun, Bendlin wanted to move like he wanted a new hole in the head.

Bendlin stood statue still and watched. Shimmering blades of swirling purple and blue flashed in the darkness. The Chimera didn't move as his slivers of solid light rose and fell like the petals of some deadly flower. Men screamed to the sounds of humming energy, swishing hither and yon as their blood splashed against floors and walls with clockwork regularity.

The smell of blood smothered every other scent in the room. The pleading confused moans of the dying wove an evil harmony to the vibrating whoosh of dozens of swinging blades. Fingers sailing east from hands soaring south hit the ground in a staccato musical rhythm that added a twisted beauty to the massacre that Bendlin couldn't help but find mesmerizing. As the slaughter went on, he began to notice complex intoxicating patterns usually only found on the lapels of formal regalia.

Bendlin searched for Crayton in the chaos. He found him nearly diced in a pile stretching a dozen feet toward Rorou's position. Perhaps he'd tried to reach him in the dark. It didn't last long, it couldn't have, but the nightmares would.

Under a power the invaders didn't understand, the light returned. Bits of men twitched and wiggled in bloody pools that once gave them life. Bendlin's tower began to fade; he could feel it bowing under his feet. He chose to hop down before it collapsed completely, and a moment later it did. He pick-stepped his way past the stringy, stinking carnage to stand next to his terrifying companion.

Rorou didn't look good. He was pale, his hair was sweat-plastered to his head, and he was huffing like he had run up a mountain. Bendlin was old enough to know not to say, "You okay?" but he was really unsure. He kept reminding himself these weren't men. They had skin and hair and appeared to be breathing but they'd never passed through the thighs of a woman. They didn't even have belly buttons!

He watched from an arm's length away, ready to jump back or stab the young man, whichever seemed more helpful in the moment. Rorou looked up at Bendlin, eyes deep-set pools of swirling energy, teeth bared in a painful grimace. Bendlin felt fear, true fear.

"You okay?" he asked anyway.

"That was intense. I'm winded," Rorou said with genuine human emotion.

Bendlin could finally see the boy that he was beneath the monster his training had made him. He was maybe twenty summers, charming and lighthearted. And at his core, tortured like no other. Bendlin extended his hand. Rorou took it and rose to his feet. The two stood there looking at each other. Bendlin felt ... uncomfortable. Rorou wore an expression he had never seen on a human face.

His eyes were half-lidded though his eyebrows were high. The corners of his mouth bent down in a frown, but his lips peeled back from his teeth in the middle, reminiscent of a smile. Bendlin could only describe it as a demon wearing a stolen halo.

"Where to?" Bendlin asked.

"A quiet spot to eat. Need to recharge. Then—"

A whistle cut the air, a long, powerful warbling sound that came from far away but was unbelievably loud.

"What in the name of a dragon's slit was that?!"

Bendlin could only shake his wide-eyed head in response. Rorou went into his pocket and pulled out a vile of Hundred-berry wine, an almost divine level healing potion. He sucked it down virulently.

Bendlin spun his Axis and set his feet. The sound reverberated far too long. It came from above. Rorou shoved the old man, not hard enough to knock him down, just hard enough to send him stumbling to the far side of the room through blood puddles and piles of innards.

The ceiling exploded inward. Stones the size of mules crashed down in a deluge of red dust and deafening crash. Rorou constructed a wall to stop the flood of dust, which broke around him like a stone in a stream. He swung his arms to the left and his wall with it, fanning the cloud away, revealing the true lord of the tower.

"No. Raptor," Bendlin whispered with heavenly horror.

Rorou stood his ground as the monster shrieked again. The room was heavy with sound. Rorou could feel his eardrums bowing under the pressure, his vision tunneling as blood vessels were squeezed in the assault but he didn't flinch. When the monster finished, he brushed the hair from his face and took a step forward.

"You ... are ... big..."

A Dragon Mantis, standing ten feet tall, twitched its mandibles as its compound eyes focused exclusively on the bold Chimera. It was almost beautiful in this land of endless white. Its body was a rich chocolate brown with vibrant patches of yellow and green. Jagged spikes covered armor thicker and harder than any shield in Fuumashon.

"A big egg is still just an egg," Rorou said, constructing a two-handed war ax.

The giant bug didn't move. With a roar, Rorou drew back, swung up, over, and down with incredible force, right between the monster's eyes. With a ceramic *clack,* his blade stopped dead on the monster's head. Painful vibrations shot up his arms through the blade.

"Shit."

Raptor released a cry and swiped at the Chimera who barely dodged in time. The healing potion would need time to work, time it didn't look like he would have. He came out of his roll and dived again. Coming to his feet, he threw his head back, going into a full backbend to avoid being beheaded by the serrated front limb of the monster. His head bounced off the ground, knees screaming in protest at the sudden stress. He rolled over; coming up wide-eyed, mouth agape. There was no way a thing that size could move that fast.

"Open to suggestions!" he shouted to Bendlin.

The old northerner was still dealing with his own trauma, an old wound he thought forever closed. Rorou rolled toward the creature as it hopped back to keep him directly in front of it. He came out of his roll, punching his palms to the sky. A razor-thin blade shot up from the floor into the "soft" underbelly of the creature with no effect.

Rorou blanched. He was off his game. That twirling blade display took more out of him than he realized. He was tired. His body was tired. His mind was tired. His constructs depended on his focus and willpower, and both were severely depleted at the moment.

Raptor lunged forward with a double pincer swipe. Rorou ran toward the insect, constructing a vaulting pole. With a vaulting somersault, he landed on the bug's back, grabbing onto thorns on its thorax for support. He straddled the bug like a horse, constructed as he swung. The blade of a climbing ax tapered down to a needle-sharp point hit between Raptor's eyes and skipped off!

"FUCK YOU, BUG! WHY DO YOU EXIST!?"

He swung again and again, doing less damage in his rage. Raptor opened its back, flapping its wings hard enough to dislodge the Chimera and send him flying. He landed awkwardly but rolled to save his ankle. He looked back in time to see a ton of insect bearing down on him.

As the creature's blades came, Rorou smiled, wondering how he was going to survive *this* time. Bendlin stabbed his blade into the creature's cloacae in a full charge, driving it in as far as his momentum would carry him. Raptor shrieked, arms going high and wide in surprised agony. Bendlin twisted left, right, and left again before back and forth in a sawing motion. Raptor flapped its wings, blowing the man over.

Rorou chuckled to himself, almost disappointed, tears rimming his eyes. With a grunt and shaky legs, he pulled himself to his feet. Bendlin's Axis was wedged in the creature's hind end, sawing deeper with every jarring movement.

"Catch!" Rorou shouted and threw nothing to Bendlin.

For reasons he would never understand, Bendlin made ready to catch even though Rorou threw nothing and had nothing to throw. A thin line appeared in the air, sailing to Bendlin's hand. With a pulse and flare, an Axis formed and slapped into his hands with familiar weight. Bendlin spun the weapon hand to hand then behind the back and around his body. He stopped it with a slap and frowned.

"Too heavy!" he shouted. The weapon pulsed and thinned a bit. Bendlin shook it. "Close enough!"

He had Raptor's full attention now. Clicking mandibles and eagerly padding feet made a terrible sound as bug adjusted in the rubble. He would need room to dance and dodge, and that pile was going to be a problem. Raptor leapt, set its wings buzzing and dive bombed the old NUUK. Bendlin back peddled, getting his spacing just right. Scythe-like limbs came down like executioner's blades. Bendlin ducked, rolled left and jumped. His swing was short and precise, clipping the monstrosity in its relatively tiny antennae.

The creature wailed, legs and feet scrambling but taking the beast nowhere as its limbs flew up to protect its injury. The Northman screamed a throat-ripping cry, shoving his blade vertically between the middle and metathorax, rowing like a man trying to escape a storm.

Rorou changed the construction; the Axis pulsed and flashed, the wide flat blade extended two more feet inside the creature, then exploded into the shape of a dandelion. Raptor leaped back to safety, taking Bendlin's second weapon with it. Raptor was wailing! A heart-stopping alien shriek disturbed the dust on the floor.

"Well done, old man! How do we finish it?"

Bendlin didn't respond. If he had, it would've only seemed cowardly to the crazy southerner. But he had hunted these things all his life. He had lost two sons, one to *this* one in particular. The truth was he didn't believe they could finish it off. But he knew he wasn't leaving that tower until one of them was dead.

Raptor dropped into a crouch, belly flat on the ground, wing-covers up as shields as it peeked between its forelimbs.

"This is how we die," the Northman said.

Wet pods lining the monster's back bubbled and burst, burping out a swarm of flying bugs. Brown-grey bugs beat their wings, flinging away the goop of their cocoons with a sick, peeling sound. Airborne, the swarm began to glow in flashes like fireflies.

Their pulses, random at first, started slowly synchronizing until they were a cloud of continuous light. The cloud went bright. With a crack of thunder, it discharged a hundred needle-thin bolts of lightning that swallowed Bendlin while he screamed.

Rorou was sweating, hoping he was fast enough. The light in the room faded back to its normal gloom and the cocky Chimera flashed a relieved smile. Bendlin stood amazed but unhurt, wrapped in a dome of protective energy.

He noticed his hands and inspected the rest of himself to find Rorou had wrapped him in resplendent purble armor. Oversized gauntlets, chainmail beneath multi-layered plate armor and a decadent helm that covered all but the man's eyes, glowed like a divine gift on the old warrior.

His head whipped toward Rorou who threw him a wink and a weak smile. Bendlin examined the armor. It was the stuff of legend. Spikes and blades covered every surface. Sigils and runes of power carved into every decorative plate, his red scaled armor beneath painted it a deeper shade than the armor around it giving it the most regal appearance he could imagine.

Bendlin hopped left, then right. The armor weighed nothing! In truth, Rorou was controlling it, syncing its movements with the man inside, not that Bendlin would ever know ... or care.

"For Brellin, you shit-eater."

The grieving father charged in silence. His footfalls crunched over crags and pebbles. The cloud pulsed again, seeking synchronicity, preparing for another blast. Bendlin didn't know if he would survive. Bendlin didn't care. The warrior was gone, replaced by a broken heart convinced vengeance would ease its pain.

The cloud fired. Blinding yellow light filled the room. Crackling lightning and barking thunder followed. Rorou heard a roar that couldn't mean anything but death.

Rorou felt the impact on his construct as he always did. Keeping light squeezed together into solid form was the equivalent of playing two separate instruments while dancing and singing in time. Keeping it together as a thousand streaks of lightning raked across it was adding a mouthful of toothaches to the mix. He grunted through the pain, forced it deep into the back of his mind and focused all his might on keeping his charge alive.

He didn't bother to open his eyes even after the heat faded and he could see again. He instead used his connection to his construct to feel what was happening beyond his eyelids. The old man was in rare form. There was almost no technique anymore. He was kicking and pulling, ripping and turning whatever it was he was holding like an animal.

He could feel the sweat against his construct. Bulging muscles quivered beyond the point of failure and somehow still flexed. There would be moments of pure tension where Bendlin was straining followed by a sudden rush of freedom as though he was pushing or pulling against something that finally gave. It went on impossibly long. The man couldn't have much more in him. Even if he were in his prime, he would be nearing the upper limits of human capability! Still, the man fought on.

The swarm began charging again. Rorou constructed a bubble around it just before discharge. The orb glowed bright blue as the swarm released its lightning storm but with nowhere for it to go, the bugs inside cooked themselves to death in a flash of poetic justice.

Rorou was exhausted. His brain was on fire. His bones ached. The fluid in his eyes felt dry and sticky. His tongue was numb and he couldn't feel his limbs anymore. With a desperate growl, he forced himself to hold on. He had promised his king, and while Chimera found it acceptable to fail in death, to fail and survive was simply failure. Failure was unacceptable.

Master Sok had often said, *"Failure is a matter of will, not completion of the task. Not completing the task is not failure, but giving up is."*

Rorou was unaware of the moment when he passed out. In his dream, he carried on serving the Northman and through him his king, but his flesh could not obey his mind. A gentle darkening closed in and swallowed him completely.

He opened his eyes to find Bendlin shoulder deep in the monster's mouth, its scythe-like forelimb sawed several inches deep in his side. Rorou's armor was long gone and the old man had pushed himself farther than any man the Chimera had ever seen, and he still continued his losing battle. He looked to be scraping inside the monster's skull with short twitchy jabs as the creature screamed. Raptor's thrashing and twisting to dislodge the pest was pointless; it wouldn't relent.

The man might have been dead for all he knew; the bug definitely *should* have been, but they continued to battle. It was beyond reason. Rorou put aside his pain and exhaustion. He put aside his sense of pride and honor. He put aside his sense of duty to his king and sunk his teeth into the infinite pool of hate that always filled that hole in his soul and he drank deeply.

Using that hate as fuel, he pulled his body up to his knees and crawled with pure bestial vitriol. He made it to the Axis still buried in the bug's backend and latched on to it. With strength born of pure negative emotion, he arched his back, flexed every muscle in his body and tore the weapon free. Gallons of thick green ooze sprayed from the wound. Rorou stayed right where he landed. The bug wheezed, deflating as if the blade had been the plug holding it all together.

Bendlin fell away from Raptor, his arm hanging like flaccid meat, and hit the ground with no resistance. Rorou watched as Raptor struggled to fight, or run or survive, just a few minutes longer and showed no emotion as it failed. The noise was unbearable; sharp pathetic squealing seeped from the creature as it finally accepted its fate. He watched it deflate and topple over. He watched it crash down and sag. He watched it darken and lie still. Then he watched until even its limbs stopped their death twitches. The broken Chimera turned his head toward the old man's broken body.

"Hey ... you okay?" he asked.

Bendlin laughed, one hearty blood-filled exhale before he devolved into a coughing fit. "That bug killed my son. King wouldn't let me kill it. When it sheds ... we use ... the pieces for armor," he choked out. He was dying, likely already dead, only his body didn't know it.

"You disobeyed your king," Rorou stated for reasons he himself couldn't explain.

"Kalmar. And I serve another now .... so ...fuck him," the disgraced NUUK said with a satisfied, blood-toothed grin.

Rorou looked at the broken pile of old man with heavy sad eyes. "You're dying," he said.

"You don't miss a thing." Bendlin responded.

"Do you want to live?" Rorou asked somberly.

Many seconds passed.

"Yes," he whispered weakly.

He died the very next breath.

Rorou closed his eyes and left his flesh. He could see the old man's soul as it escaped into the either. He grabbed hold with a strength his flesh would never possess and drew him in.

"Where are we?"

"We haven't gone far. Look down."

"Is that my body?"

"What's left of it," he said with a chuckle.

"Am I dead?"

"Yes. But it's not permanent. If you want to go back ... you can."

Bendlin looked at the frail pile of flesh lying in a heap on the ground, already starting to freeze. He couldn't believe how old he looked.

"Is that what people see when they look at me?!" he wondered, and suddenly many, many things in his life made sense.

He understood why his years of knowledge and service did not grant him the respect he had earned. He understood why he was called to stand by the throne rather than on the wall, where he made his name to begin with. He looked ... useless, and it cut deeper than he ever could have believed.

"You would be crippled, likely severely, but you would be alive."

Bendlin looked at him. This was unbelievable. To think that there were beings with this kind of power simply walking the earth, looking like everyone else. What else was out there, beyond those frozen peaks? How much more didn't he know? How had he ever been satisfied with his simple thoughtless life?

"Send me back," he said sternly.

The look in his eyes bordered on threatening.

Rorou smiled. "Let's go have some fun."

"Let's!"

8

...BAND BACK TOGETHER

"War paves the way for peace. Peace plants the seeds of war."

Shefa limped out of the lower east tower as flames engulfed it and a chorus of hundreds screamed inside its baking walls. Rorou and Bendlin marched from the west tower as the ruckus of collapsing floors and a cloud of dust chased them into the waning sunlight. Rorou threw a wave; Shefa threw one back. They approached each other at an even clip, but Dridden slowed as they got closer.

"What magic is this?" he whispered to Shefa who only shook his head in response.

The Northmen grasped forearms but didn't smile.

"More than northern blood in you, too, I see," Bendlin said with an uncomfortable smile.

They examined each other warily. Dridden was a monster of a man. He seemed to have grown half a foot and his hair was a shade of red that simply didn't exist in the Whitelands. His muscles bulged and twitched with even the slightest motion, promising strength only heard of in legends. His massive paw wrapped around his Axis like a child's toy, but his transformation was hardly noteworthy next to Bendlin's.

Chimera blood was an almost magical thing. It was conjured by magic, imbued with magic and maintained more than a pinch of the power that brought it into being. Rorou had given the man a transfusion significant enough to save his broken flesh, then continued to share his blood until the power it carried beat back the ravages of war and time.

The sixty-year-old man who left only a few hours before was no more, replaced by a younger version with no grey hair, wrinkles, or old wounds slowing him down. Rorou, on the other hand, looked like shit. He was thin and pale, couldn't stand upright, and that cocky twinkle in his eyes was whittled down to a barely existent sheen.

"Too much fun?"

"Ha, guess it does exist. You said bring him back. I bringed him back."

"Did you say bringed?"

"Did I?"

Shefa stared at his clanmate. He looked at him truly, deeper than flesh and bravado, and could see the light that shined within all Chimera was dangerously dim in him.

"Call him."

Rorou scoffed. "And admit I need his help? Think I'd rather die."

"I'm sure you would, but if it were about you, Raymond's guest suite would never be empty."

"Truer words were never spoken," he said with a strained chuckle.

Noise in the distance drew their attention. It was a subtle thing, hovering just below the howl of the wind and the roar of the flames, but it was unmistakable.

"Troop movement."

"Agreed. So, was that a test or did it take that long for word to spread?"

A sharp whistle cut through every other sound. The Chimera looked up to highest window in the main keep, a fifteen story monster of a tower. A figure stood there looking back.

"Well, they know we're here now. No more half measures will do," Shefa said with an exhausted sigh.

"Sheath—" Rorou started

"Don't," Shefa cut him off, adamant.

"Fuck you," Rorou shot back.

Shefa turned on him, cold-fire rage burning in his eyes.

Rorou's muscles were clenched so tight his body was quivering. "We check you. That's our role, that's what we do. You run off half-cocked like some sort of invincible hero and we clean up the mess. And there's always a mess. So, no. Fuck you, shut up, this is what we're doing."

"I—" Shefa started but Rorou cut him off.

"I WAS THERE! I watched them fall, same as you. Not *your* friends, not *your* clanmates, OURS! You are first among us but you are still among us. Not above. Not more than."

Shefa didn't move. He wanted to fight, he wanted to win. He started to throw the fact that Rorou didn't want to admit that he needed help back in his face. He played the argument out in his mind, what he would say, how Rorou would respond. Point and counter-point until one of them yielded. In every scenario he could think of, Rorou was right and he hated that.

Shefa didn't break eye contact as he reached into the extra-dimensional pouch at the small of his back. He pulled out Aurohra, his dragon-scale gauntlet. He stared at it with something between fear and lust. It was a gift from his friend and former master, Garrison. It was gifted to him by Shefa's mother, the emerald mistress, Emmafuumindall.

Wearing it connected him to her, and through her, incredible power. But it made him much more dragon than he was comfortable with. Twice as much power, half as much humanity. Sorrow, fear, compassion, all smothered under an ocean of self-love and pride. It had helped him defeat every foe to ever stand before him but it also gave him an unquenchable thirst for power and dominance.

Rorou snapped his fingers. Shefa looked up at him.

"It's time, Sheath," Rorou said.

Shefa nodded, sadly, slowly.

"Sunrise," he said, as he made off for the first tower.

The party returned to the Dwarven ritual circle in the main keep. They shuffled in tentatively but Shefa made it clear they were following him with or without their consent. Shefa extended his hands, inviting them to join him and hold hands for whatever reason. They obliged.

"Dwarven magic is not like Elvin magic. The principle is the same but the execution is different. Dwarves see magic as a tool. Elves see magic as air, a necessity. It is everywhere in all things at all times," Shefa explained.

Bendlin gave a smart nod, though he had no idea what Shefa's point was. Dridden was openly perplexed.

"The carvings in the walls don't cancel magic, they absorb it. Any magic summoned within these walls is sucked up and stored here. This is what animates the dead, creates and sustains the gargoyles. Each signature carved into the walls is a contract. It allows them to access the power stored here while siphoning a tiny bit from each in case of a drought."

Shefa summoned a small pulse of arcane energy and spread it through the group. The Northmen tensed at the unexpected sensation. They could feel an electric worm crawling through them, searching for imperfections to restore.

Bendlin looked at Shefa, confused. "If the names are the only ones who can access this power, how are you doing it?"

"Because my father's name is on the wall," he said with a nod across the way.

"Rocksaw?" Rorou asked.

"Better. Gromble." Rorou smiled, and the Northmen shrugged at each other. "We heal, we eat, we rest. Sunrise, we finish this."

"And what is to keep them from killing us in the night?" Dridden asked.

"Me," Shefa said curiously.

"So we sleep in shifts, then."

"No need," both Chimera said.

"He doesn't sleep," Rorou offered, hooking a thumb at Shefa.

"I'll lead you through the meditation. Lay down." They obliged, heads to the center of the circle so they could still hold hands. "Breathe. Carefully. Controlled. In for one beat, out for three."

The group followed Shefa's lead. The Northmen thought it silly but after seeing the power this youth could wield, they decided to play along. If there was even a chance that this ridiculous hoo-doo would work, they wanted to reap the rewards. After five cycles of breathing, they started to feel more relaxed.

"Clear your mind. Think of black. Infinite nothingness stretching forever in every direction. Now picture yourself in the center of it. No sound. No light. Nothing but you surrounded by nothing and the sound of my voice."

Dridden felt the tension in his body melt, running like drops off an icicle in the afternoon sun. His back fell flat against the floor. His were feet drifting away from each other as the threats surrounding them faded from memory.

"Now, build. Create a single star in that endless black. A single point twinkling in an empty black sky. Now build another. And another. Fill your sky with stars. One hundred, one million, legions uncountable until the dark is tiny spaces between the light you have made. Now structure those stars. Each one is made of heavenly power, pure starlight. They bring light and life. Heat and warmth. Each one containing enough power to fill your body a thousand times over. Can you feel that power?"

"Yes," Bendlin said in a holy whisper.

Dridden was too overcome to speak. Rorou smiled. It tickled him every time Shefa reminded him why he was first among them.

"Now, consume. Picture each star, shooting across the heavens to you. Every twinkling light, every heavenly body seeking your flesh. See them pierce your body and join the light inside you. Feel them die, each one giving its life to bolster yours. Every ache dulled. Every wound healed. Every memory returned. Feel the stars fill you with joy and hope, power and patience. Youth and vigor are yours. Strength beyond exhaustion, focus beyond fear, you are the best possible version of yourself. Light is your sustenance; you no longer need food. Nature is your companion; you no longer need friends. You are all that you want. You are all that you need. Your will is all that exists. Now open your eyes and be reborn."

Dridden opened his eyes and felt tears streak down his cheeks. He didn't know when he'd started crying and more confusing, he didn't know why. He felt different. Still him, but changed, as if he had gone through a second childhood and became a man all over again.

He felt ... sustained. Whole. As if a piece of him he didn't know was missing had suddenly been returned and snapped into place. He sat up, looking for Shefa. He was gone. Bendlin sat up next, eyes running like rivers but the once-old-now-young man didn't wipe them; he let them be.

"Where is Shefa?" Bendlin asked.

"He left half an hour ago," Rorou answered.

"Half of an hour?! How long have when been here?!"

Rorou didn't answer, just pointed to the sky. The sun was gone. The light from the symbols on the floor cast the sky a gorgeous swirl of lavender and blue. Frosted clouds stretched across the heavens like the first smears of paint on an empty canvas, wispy salamanders drifting on invisible currents with no destination in mind. It was the kind of beauty that men who bathe in blood forget to appreciate. Dridden felt his eyes water again.

Bendlin noticed Rorou had gotten his color back; he still seemed tired, but not on death's door like he did before. He searched for Shefa. He wandered back to the Grinder, wondering if he was there eating more rancid meat.

He searched the frozen wastes for signs of life. He didn't see any movement. He didn't see any footprints in the snow. He felt the cold bite at him and remembered how frigid it was beyond that chamber. A faint whistling drew his eyes up. A shadow blocked out the moon. His instincts told him to move.

He jumped back, as a boulder the size of a house sailed past and crashed into the ice with an explosive crystalline retort. Chips of ice flew everywhere, daggers hidden in a cloud of blooming snow as the boulder itself shattered into hundreds of chunks, each one big enough to kill a man.

A few heartbeats later, a second boulder rained down, not as big as the first but still larger than any man could move. It landed with a similar effect. He waited for a third to whistle down; instead, Shefa sailed down from the roof as if on his own personal cloud.

The jewel in the ring on his finger shined brighter than any star in the sky; the jewels on his armor gleamed likewise. The sockets where his eyes should have been spewed a dense emerald fog that trailed behind him like comet tails.

"I needed to refresh my stores."

Bendlin noted the choir of voices, as if several people spoke his words. It made the hairs on the back of his neck stand up. He thought to lighten the mood with a joke.

"You didn't eat anything out there, did you?

"I ate everything out there," Shefa said, walking past without slowing.

Bendlin noticed Shefa's uniform was much cleaner now. His wounds were all healed, the bags under his eyes gone. What must it be like, not to know such power, but to never have known otherwise. Bendlin thought often of the gods, his culture had hundreds of them. He often wondered how sweet life would be if he could take or do anything he wanted and no one could stop him. If this boy was any indication, not sweet at all.

He stopped in the center of the ritual circle, threw his head back and went statue still. That strip of white hair swayed in the breeze, making him seem more statuesque somehow. Bendlin watched for a moment. Sixty years of hard living taught him that if you wait long enough, your questions will be answered without ever needing to be asked. Shefa's voice appeared in his head.

"Wondering what I'm doing?"

Bendlin started. It was a jarring thing to have someone speak into your thoughts.

"I figured if I watched long enough, I could figure it out for myself."

"Would you like to see?"

Nothing.

"Well?"

"See what?"

"What I see?"

"I might not have star glass peepers like you, but these old eyes work good enough. Especially now."

Inside his mind, Shefa chuckled. *Do you really think I see with my eyes?*

Bendlin decided to lie. He hated feeling foolish but Shefa saved him from having to.

"I'm in your mind; you can't lie to me any more than you can lie to yourself."

"Well, now you know I'm scared witless of any more of your skull sorcery."

"Mind magic. Relax your mind. Listen to my thoughts, my heart. You *know* I would die twice before I let any harm come to you."

Bendlin could feel the truth of his words. The conviction of his promise was in whatever bond they now shared. But the fear would not abate.

Shefa was thirty feet from him. The young king pointed at Bendlin, much too far away to touch him, but he felt that finger on his skin, right in the center of his forehead. It was as if a cage holding all his worries shattered, and his fears flew away like a flock of startled crows. He turned calm, awestruck eyes on Shefa who still stood thirty feet away, now holding out his hand, offering it to the old warrior. With a faith in his heart, Bendlin crossed the distance and took the Chimera's hand.

The world fell away. He watched as the ground shot away from his feet. His stomach crawled up into his throat. It was as if a giant bird had scooped him up and hurled him into the sky. He couldn't feel his legs but he was sure he must've wobbled on his feet. A heartbeat later they were standing in a place the Northman couldn't have guessed with a million tries.

"This is my quiet place. You are inside my mind."

Bendlin looked around. Infinite black bejeweled with uncountable stars. Not just the silver twinkles he had observed all his life but dancing gems that sparkled in every conceivable color. There was no floor, yet something solid beneath his feet allowed him to stand.

"I thought that was just some monk hoo-doo, you know, to clear the mind or something."

"Do I seem like the type to participate in hoo-doo?"

"No, no you do not."

Shefa pointed. "That star there, the blue one? That is the world you know. Earth."

"I ... I don't understand."

"You look up every night and see the stars; what do you think your world would look like if you stood on one of them? Every star you see is a world as full and rich as the one you know. This is where Rorou goes. This is how we see the world, one tiny twinkle in an endless sea. We know how little our actions mean in the grand scheme of things, so we focus on the little things. Our family, our friends, our home. That's what we allow to matter. Care about too much and you'll always be miserable."

Bendlin opened his eyes and found he was lying on the floor at Shefa's feet. Rorou and Dridden were lost in the deepest sleep. Dridden was snoring like he wanted to break his own nose. The old warrior looked up at Shefa who appeared to not have moved a muscle. He searched the sky; he had lost at least an hour. He rolled over onto his back, made a pillow of his arms and watched the stars between the clouds.

Sometime later, what passed for sunlight crept over the peaks of the frozen mountaintops. Dridden's tree sawing caught and stuttered before he groggily made his way to the land of the waking. Shefa still hadn't moved.

Rorou spoke without moving. "Are you putting the damn glove on?"

Bendlin looked over. Was he talking to him? The prince was still squinting against the sunlight. He waited, unsure what to do.

"Yes," Shefa said simply.

He turned his head down from the sky, rolling it left and right to a symphony of cracks and pops. Rorou tapped Bendlin on the shoulder and bade him to follow with a jerk of his head. He moved quickly and quietly. The Chimera grabbed the prince by the scruff of his armor and dragged him along behind. They stopped against the wall, away from the wind but catching what little sun they could.

"What's the story with the 'damn glove'?" Bendlin whispered.

"The gauntlet that he looks at like a wild viper is a gift from his mother, a true ancient dragon. Wearing it makes him ... dangerous."

"Wait, *wearing it* makes him dangerous? What the hell is he now?"

"Cold. Empty. He's searching for purpose, something to fill the void inside him, but there is no malice there. That thing makes him an animal. Half as likely to kill us as them ... if he wears it too long."

Bendlin rolled that around. It wasn't much but it was a lot. Power at the cost of his soul. *Him* ... MORE powerful. What would that even look like?

"If it is as dangerous as you say, why not just throw it away and be done with it?"

Rorou made to slap the old man across the face. *"Throw it away?!* Devil's taint, man! First, it's a gift, from his mother. Second, will your blade cut you as cleanly as your foes? Do you throw *it* away, or do you learn to master it?" Rorou shook his head, disgusted.

"It was just a question."

"You have no idea. None. That boy has gone to war with Heaven and Hell. Angels, demons, beings of pure light have died in his hands and each took a part of him with them. He asked for none of this. He did what he had to and you are alive and well today because of the nightmares he has taken into himself."

Bendlin looked into the wild eyes of the youth standing before him. He didn't see anger or rage there. He saw sorrow. As if he wished he could end his friend's suffering but the fates would not be so kind. He was hurting. An old wound, and one that would likely never heal. A situation Bendlin knew all too well. He needed a distraction, he needed the fire in those eyes to flare and burn out. Anything just then would be better than that haunted stare.

"So how do we keep him from killing us while he's killing them?"

Rorou seemed to deflate, all emotion weeping from him in an instant, replaced by the cocky kid without a care in the world. "Same as all weapons; point the dangerous end *that* way," he said with a self-assured smirk and an obnoxious wink.

Bendlin turned his eyes back to Shefa who held that gauntlet in his hands like a baby dragon, prone to turn and destroy him without reason or warning. Gleaming like jewelry, it was said to come from a great emerald dragon, and while he didn't believe in dragons having never seen one himself, at that moment it at least seemed possible.

Shefa pulled his tool from his belt, a deep purple cylinder that might have been a sword handle once. Though metal, it flowed like liquid in his hands, going from perfectly smooth to a fair-sized dagger. Shefa pulled the blade along his forearm, opening a wound six inches long. He didn't grunt. His face never twitched a muscle. As sparkling blood ran down his arm, he took the gauntlet in his right hand and slammed it onto his left with a roar.

Emerald light exploded, filling the space. Bendlin closed his eyes at the sting and found it still burned through his eyelids. He covered his face with his hand and could feel his forearm starting to sweat from the heat. Then it was gone.

Shefa stood there, his cloak whipping wildly in a phantom breeze the others couldn't feel. The scales from the gauntlet crawled up his arm as though fusing itself to his body, no longer a thing he wore but wholly a part of him.

He flashed his teeth in a silent threat. No longer white but grey, like good steel. His body didn't change but he became more ferocious, more imposing, even at that distance. The light show sputtered out and the Shefa he knew was there once more.

"If you have food, eat. When the sun clears that middle peak, damnation."

BLOOD STORM

"I never bluff. When I draw my blade, I use it exactly as its creator intended."

Across the courtyard between the burnt-out husk of the lower west tower and the pile of rubble that was the east, stood an army. No gaggle of sellswords or band of mercenaries; these were men and women who trained day and night, lived and breathed war and survived by being experts at their craft. Men patrolled the entryway, guards manned the door. Archers ringed the upper layers, strung bows in hand.

Through the front door was a tight hall, likely filled with traps and doom; beyond that, barricades to halt enemy progress. They didn't have uniforms but they had discipline. Not one was sleepy or unalert; none would be caught off guard. This wasn't a band striking out to harass towns and villages; this was something more.

It takes a fortune to marshal an army. Men need weapons, armor, food, entertainment. Most nations went broke funding their wars. Someone powerful, wealthy, and above all clever, was behind this. Someone formidable.

"What's the plan? There is a plan, right? Tell me there's a plan," Bendlin said.

"Yes, there is a plan," Shefa promised.

Bendlin released a monster sigh. "Good. What's the plan?"

Shefa smirked. "I'm going to ask them to surrender."

He marched out into the open. A thousand eyes fell on him instantly; he could feel them like bugs on his skin. As he left the safety of the courtyard, the wind hit him like a wave of knives, frigid claws raking across his flesh as though his armor was a lie.

His inner ears ached immediately. As he closed on the front rank of soldiers, shields came up and swords slid free. Shefa stopped far enough away for them to feel safe. *Feel* safe. Shefa had donned the gauntlet; no one was safe.

"Who am I speaking to?"

He raised his voice to the window where he'd saw the mysterious figure yesterday. A man broke formation; tall, well built, dressed in heaping layers of leather and fur. Not from these parts.

"I am—"

Shefa interrupted him with a *KINSPEAR* right through his open mouth. The crowd reeled and shuddered as his head exploded, covering them in brains and blood. The man's body stood there, dying for a time, spurting blood from its neck flaps before gravity finally took it down. Shocked and hate-filled faces stared at him over raised shields, silver and white affairs bearing a crest he didn't know; a ruby surrounded by a golden ring.

"Who am I speaking to?" he said again.

A husky voice responded. "Who are you to question me, here in my home?" Husky, but definitely female.

"I come on behalf of Kalmar Grond. These are his lands. Order will be restored. I won't kill any more than I have to."

The voice laughed, not mockingly, but almost surprised, as if it didn't know the laugh was coming. "You will kill and kill and kill some more. That's what you do. It's what you are."

Shefa wasn't sure how to proceed. This person knew him, more than he was comfortable with. Had his legend reached the top of the world? No, none in town or the castle knew him. This was an old foe. Someone he'd failed to kill before, perhaps?

"The killing will stop. The raids will stop. Tell me what you want, let me help you get it so that you, your people, and the people of the Whitelands can go back to their peaceful, miserable snow sucking lives."

The voice was silent for a while. The lull in conversation reminded him how cold he was. Something told him to wait, so he did.

"I want you," the voice came back.

Shefa fixed his mouth to respond several times before he found the word he would ultimately use. "WHAT?!"

"You. Give yourself to me; swear fealty and loyalty to me. Kneel and kiss my boot and I will leave your villages in peace."

"Okay," Shefa said without hesitation.

"Also, you will follow my every order without question or hesitation."

"You want me as your ... slave?"

Shefa stared up at the shadow. The shadow silently stared back.

"Yes."

"You understand that if we can't come to some arrangement, I'm going to kill all of you, yes?"

"I believe you believe that. I believe you'll try."

Shefa thought for a minute. He looked at the humans gathered before him, wheat before his scythe. Killing them would make little difference. He already saw the faces of those he'd killed whenever he closed his eyes; what are one hundred more faces amidst a sea of millions?

"I didn't want this."

"Yes, you did."

Shefa started walking toward the enemy line. A volley of arrows leaped from their bows, screaming through the frozen air for his heart. He continued walking, unconcerned. The red and green sashes tied around his arms bent light, making him seem to be standing either left or right of his true location. The arrows missed by an embarrassing stretch.

As they came in range, the *KINSTONES* on his armor flared, sapping their kinetic energy. Score upon score of metal-tipped death shafts clattered on the ice around him. He could hear the archers nocking their bows. He continued walking.

"Snow Hawks! Fold!" a young man in the front row belted.

The straight line of soldiers before him bent like a bow, forming a half-circle around him, threatening to encompass him as he approached. He stopped in the center of their formation. It was too cold to sweat but he could smell their fear. Fear was a bad sign; sane men fear. Fearless and fool were often one and the same. It was easy to kill fools.

"Snow Hawks, collapse!"

The men raised their shields and pressed forward, one careful step at a time and in perfect unity. The huff of their breathing and the synchronized crunch of ice was a haunting sound. The squinted eyes and plumes of breath cresting their shields was a fearsome sight. This is what a final vision was supposed to look like. They would die proud of themselves, Shefa thought.

"Kartanis, finish it."

A brave young man stepped forward. Large, handsome, some beautiful lass likely waiting for him at home. He wore not only leather and furs but the red insect shells that the Kalmar's knights wore. He was careful. Steady behind his shield. The man moved into range, measuring his target.

With a lightning quick slash, he brought his blade down on the center of Shefa's head. His KINSTONES flared and the man's blade gently kissed his hair. Shefa slapped the weapon out of the man's hand and snatched him close.

He whispered, "Stay in the back, fall early. Better a coward than a corpse."

"Snow Hawks, move!" the young man shouted.

Shefa snapped his boot into the brave man's shin, just hard enough to break it. He threw the man over the ring soldiers, not bothering to listen for his landing; he had seen this show too many times before.

Blades came at him like rain. He stepped into them, arms wide, eyes closed. He felt the cold kiss of iron as they fell like feathers on his skin. His KINSTONES pulsed with power. With the slightest twitch, he released a dome of obliterating force. The men, their shields, and their armor flattened into a singular bloody mass for just a moment before they shot away from him, kites made of liquid meat.

He turned his head to the brave young man. He saw him buried under the ruin of his friends. He was in shock. Nothing he'd seen had prepared him for this. But he was alive. Shefa had done his good deed for the day.

He let out a long, slow whistle that clipped off sharp at the end. Shefa looked up at the row of archers recovering from the blast, training their arrows on him. He counted as they died. One, two, three ... ten ... fourteen, fifteen ... sixteen.

One unfortunate fellow toppled over the railing, screaming as he plunged. He hit the ice with a wet crunch and spread wide as a bed sheet, a purble arrow protruding from his hip. Shefa threw a lazy wave at Rorou and waited for them to catch up. The figure in the window and the voice that belonged to it were nowhere to be found.

Rorou and the Northmen stopped beside him.

"Some plan," Bendlin said sarcastically.

Shefa didn't respond.

"Divide and conquer?" Rorou asked. None of his usual glee was in his words.

"No. I'm tired. Chimera?"

"Hoough!" Shefa and Rorou shouted. "NUUK?"

"Hoough!" the Northmen responded with more confusion than confidence.

In a calm smooth voice Shefa said, "Forward, march."

They passed through the building, into the darkened hall where they found no resistance. As the opening on the far side crept closer, they could hear orders being given. Not "arrows," not "swords"... crank.

"Hug the wall!" Shefa shouted.

That same second, a twang like a ten-ton crossbow ripped through the air. Shefa put his hands out before him, thumbs and index fingers nearly touching. A ballista bolt large enough to kill a dragon rushed down the hall. His *KINSTONES* bled light!

One on his armor shattered in a squealing whine that set his teeth on edge. A deep resounding steel clang accompanied the bolt to the ground. Shefa was so supercharged he was vibrating in place.

"G-g-get y-your wep-wep-wep-ons ready-dy!" Shefa strained against a universal force that was trying to tear him apart. "GO!"

Rorou took a single step then vanished from sight.

"Bendlin! Go!"

Bendlin stepped forward and vanished into the light.

"Prince! GO!"

Dridden stepped forward but his foot didn't hit the ground. He soared forward, a dozen feet before he ever started to descend. When his foot did hit the ground, it was in dream-slow motion. He felt every pound as it came down on his foot. He could feel each muscle flex to absorb and disperse the impact. His hair was straight back, the hide of a porcupine, and tears streaked the sides of his face. He immediately went into a controlled slide. He surfed along the ice for thirty feet before coming to a stop.

He looked at Bendlin who was moving fast and slow at the same time. It didn't make sense. Rorou had fashioned himself a flail and was at that moment swinging it without resistance through a man's face. The man's head took a lifetime to come apart. Dridden saw every crack and wrinkle spread across his face as the conjured weapon made room for itself the man's skull. Dridden looked at the soldiers, grim men, veterans of war, and they were totally silent.

One man was jumping but he didn't move; he hung there as though frozen in time. Bendlin swung his Axis slowly, a slash that an addled child could avoid but the woman he swung at just stared at the killing blow as it opened her up from collarbone to kneecap.

She peeled open like a flower. Blood bloomed in the space where there used to be flesh, rushing out of her like juice from over-ripe fruit. He watched confusion take root in her eyes as her body told her brain things it couldn't understand.

"Prince! Kill!" Shefa said, running up behind.

He covered fifteen feet in a stride, moving both too fast and too slow to be real. Dridden watched the southern king go through twenty men like a plague. That strange purple blade was twenty feet long and where he swung it, one man became two.

"Well, if they're just going to stand there..."

Dridden rushed into the fray. He swung his blade to bat aside a man's sword and watched the man's hand shatter like crystal as the weapon sang and ever-so-slowly flew away. He watched the blade for a second, finally understanding what had happened. When Rorou disappeared, when Bendlin disappeared, they didn't vanish; they were moving too fast to see!

Was he moving that fast? Dridden picked a new target. The blade went through the man's helm, face, and neck without so much as a jerk of resistance. Seconds ticked by before the sound of the strike ever blossomed into existence.

He watched in muted horror as the young man's bright green eye blinked too slowly to close before he died. He saw blood seeking veins no longer there, spread in a spray of crimson rubies, checkering the scene behind them. His brains pumped clear fluid out onto the frozen breeze. He saw the exact moment man becomes meat and howled with sadistic glee.

A part of him was excited; the rest of him was terrified at wielding this kind of power. He thought back to every moment when punching Shefa in the face seemed like a good idea and said a silent prayer to whatever gods stayed his hand.

The four of them moved through the enemy ranks, mowing down men by the handful. Over his initial shock, Dridden went to work. He didn't swing hard; he didn't need to; a nick would open a man wide. Necks became prime targets. Throats peeled apart, heads flew free in a swirling spiral of surprised expressions and deflating torsos. Racing hearts forced their necks to spray blood like a sneeze as they died without ever knowing they fought.

It didn't take long.

Sixty men were reduced to leaking bags in as many seconds. When it was over, when none who stood against them still stood, the world slowly crept back to its usual pace and all he had done came back in a mad rush. Dridden felt a weight pressing down on him; a bone-deep weariness settled on his shoulders, trying to grind him into the earth.

"Whew! I'm winded. Feel like I've run up a mountain," he got out through painful breaths. His joints ached, and his lungs were on fire, the deep stinging burn of touching hot metal.

"Well, what do you expect? You move like that, you gotta feel the better part of dead when it's over," Bendlin explained to him, trying his best to appear not dead on his feet.

"You will balance out soon. You only burned off the extra I gave you. Almost popped a nut back there," Shefa griped.

Rorou burst into laughter; the other two followed, chuckling as hard as their exhaustion would allow.

"I don't know what's next. If you two wanna stay here and make sure they don't outflank me—" Shefa started.

"Fuck you," Bendlin interrupted. Shefa's eyes flashed green; every hair on the old man's body stood up straight but he didn't back down. "You want to leave me with the horses? Like a child or an invalid?"

There was hurt in the old man's eyes. Anger, but also hurt. Shefa hadn't thought what it must be like, to be old in a world of warriors. Nothing but sorrow and pity when people looked at you. Underappreciated, underestimated, unwanted, just ... tolerated. A living Hell for a warrior born.

"I promised to get you out of this frozen hellhole and I don't mean to carry your corpse."

"Better to die a man than live as a burden."

Shefa nodded once, sharply. The warrior visibly relaxed. One never know how challenging a dragon might end.

"Whatever comes next is ready for us. Roo and I will take point. Bendlin, left flank. Prince, right. Don't forget to look up and always, always, always..."

"WATCH YOUR STEP," the Chimera said in unison.

Shefa shook his head; Rorou grinned.

The final tower was a beast, twice as large around as any of the other two combined. The first six stories had no windows, likely dungeon cells. Windows and balconies higher up, officer's quarters and criminals of import. The top floor had bricked up windows, almost certainly booby-trapped. They would have to take the long slow road from the bottom, so be it.

The main floor of the keep was pitch black. No lamps or torches.

"Roo."

"Got it."

A purble orb appeared, throwing dreamy light a dozen feet around the room. It wasn't much, but Shefa could feel the humans relax. Damn, humans. Not Northmen, not NUUK and prince; humans. The gauntlet was affecting him. He picked up the pace.

The room was grand, large and wide with a needlessly high ceiling. He could tell by the air currents that there were tables and chairs beyond the orb's light. There once were windows but they had been bricked over, wind whistled in through cracks in the mortar. Must be a dining hall for visitors. The path in front of him was often used; he could feel the grooves in the stone.

He stopped at the stairs. Raised a hand, made a fist. Everyone halted and went church mouse quiet.

Rorou entered his mind. *"I feel it, too."*

Shefa tore a fistful of stone from the wall and tossed it in a gentle arc up the stairs. The rock hit with a loud, sharp clack in the darkness and tumbled noisily down the stairs. They listened intently as the chunks cascaded back down, waiting for a clue.

Five steps up a series of blades, six inches long, punched up from the stair and just as quickly returned to their sinister hiding place. He could hear a domino effect happening on other stairs higher up around the bend beyond view. Shefa had to admire the simple effectiveness of such a trap.

He turned to Rorou and made a leg. The leg was returned. Rorou constructed a second set of stairs over the first and they simply walked up.

"I would have just levitated us if not for these stupid stones," Shefa whined in Rorou's mind.

"They're not."

"What?"

"No stones here. You can't feel that?!"

Shefa stopped. The Northmen froze, on their guard. Shefa snapped his fingers and a green flame appeared in the space between them, gone as quick as the sound. It started low, a deep-chested rumbling. It sounded more like indigestion than anything else.

Then the cackle started, the slow rolling heckle of a madman. With a start, Shefa burst into howl-at-the-moon laughter. He looked at Rorou with tears in his wild wide eyes; he hadn't laughed like that for far too long.

"Rorou mon Albright!" he boomed like a circus ringmaster.

"Sheath Alzannananabarrenor-Fuumindall!" Rorou returned with just as much enthusiasm.

Shefa's voice dropped three octaves. "Let's go have some fun."

With that, they tore up the stairs. When they reached the top, Rorou's construct disappeared and dropped them back on the stone. The Chimera rushed around the corner with childish glee.

Dridden started to follow, but Bendlin grabbed him by the arm, shaking his head with the sternest of faces and most desperate of pleas. Bendlin waited, worried. From around the bend, he saw a flash of light and heard the flesh-eating *whoosh* of a giant fireball. Screams followed immediately.

Listening was almost as bad as watching. He could almost see the sizzling lightning, the shattering of stone and the traumatized faces of the dying. Something heavy, *very* heavy hit the floor so hard it shook the tower and half the screaming wafting downstairs stopped. The stench of burning flesh and hot metal choked the hall while the southerners slayed scores of men in stoic silence. Bendlin and Dridden waited awkwardly for the psychopaths from the south to have their massacre.

"All clear," one of them said; Bendlin couldn't tell who.

He started down the hall, disturbed by what he expected to find. The worst part of a battle, the thing that sticks with you the longest, is the smell. Second to that are the sounds. Every step closer notched the volume a tick higher.

The coughing and grunting of dying men. That sucking sound in the back of the throat as the fight against drowning in their own snot was lost. The wailing of those in too much pain to form words. But worst of all, the pleas. The begging of the vanquished to the victors for comfort and mercy. The young boys who thought themselves men, praying to absent gods in the hour of their death.

Bendlin closed his eyes. He didn't want to see. He kept them closed through the chit-chat, the plan making and pats on the back. He even held on to Dridden's sleeve as they crossed the floor.

He had seen enough horrors done in the name of kings and honor. He had heard enough honey-sweet noble lies that left boys rent to ruin by other boys too vile to know better. Here, in the autumn of his life, such things held nothing of value for him.

They came off the stairs on the third floor. Double doors separated the stairs from the landing proper. On the other side, they heard nothing. Shefa stopped at the door; his hand wouldn't reach for the handle. He looked back at Rorou.

"Trust it," was all the handsome Chimera said.

Shefa stretched his hands out before him, fingers splayed, thumbs and index fingers nearly touching. The *KINBLAST* turned the door into shrapnel. The boom alone would've half-killed anyone on the other side.

They rushed in behind the explosion, fanning out to cover every angle of the room. The smoke thinned, revealing the silhouette of a monster. It must've had three heads, eleven arms, and too many legs to count. The dust settled, revealing something worse. Much worse.

"Fuck me. Kasik the Violator," Bendlin sighed

Kasik stood nine feet tall. He was nearly as wide at the shoulders. He wore a single garment that looked like a long nightshirt lashed around the waist with a knotted chain. He wore an iron mask that appeared to be bolted to his skull with a mouth hole crusted over with filth from him shoveling too-big food through. Two vertical eye slits stole any resemblance of humanity from his appearance.

Every limb was powerfully chiseled, but the most concerning thing about this man, if it was indeed a man, was his weapon of choice. Slung over his right shoulder was a statue, life size, of a knight on horseback, sword raised to signal a charge. It must have weight a literal ton, but he didn't seem to notice its weight at all.

"And who the hellfire is Kasik the Violator?" Rorou asked

"A madman. He was put here because we couldn't figure out how to kill him," Bendlin explained.

"His crime?"

"Let's call it ... murder."

"Murder? He's in here for murder? Is that all? Who did he kill?"

"Every man, woman, and child in twelve villages. The coroner listed the offense as death by sodomy."

Rorou screwed up his face something ghastly. "Backdoor delivery ... to death? All the gods in Hell!"

Shefa started forward.

"Careful, you can't hurt him!" Bendlin called out.

"We'll see," Shefa said to himself.

He aimed his finger and fired a *KINSPEAR* dead at the man's heart. As the beam hit, Shefa flew backward down the hall. Surprised, the blow knocked the wind out of him. The *KINSTONES* in his armor absorbed kinetic energy from moving objects, but they were useless against pure force. They needed mass.

He lay on the ground writhing. He had forgotten what it was he was doing to people. Dying felt like a very reasonable option at that moment.

"Getting cocky again, hmm?" Rorou mocked.

Shefa was in too much pain to respond. Rorou turned to Bendlin

"So how do we kill him?"

"I just said we never figured it out! Maybe ... starve him to death, I don't know! I just know you can't hurt him without hurting yourself. And you still don't hurt him at all." Bendlin enacted the most violent shrug the Chimera had ever seen.

"I guess we'll have to get creative."

He constructed a glaive, a type of pole arm weapon, three feet of handle, three feet of blade. Recklessly, he charged. Kasik watched. When he got in range, Rorou threw the weapon, a perfect shot that would've put the tip in the man's right eye. Kasik watched. Rorou dismissed the construct just before impact but it worked to draw the man's attention.

Rorou dropped into a slide on his knees, leaning all the way back to make his profile as low as possible and sailed between the man's legs. Clear, he hopped onto the man's back, constructing a garrote as he flew. He snapped the thin wire around the man's neck and pulled for all he was worth.

As the wire cut into the man's neck, Rorou felt the pain of his skin splitting. He continued to pull but Kasik showed no signs of discomfort. He gave a quick flex of his back and dislodged Rorou who hit the ground and rolled to safety, hand clutching his injured neck.

Kasik hoisted the statue off his shoulder and swung it into the ceiling in one smooth motion. The ceiling came down like an avalanche and there was nowhere Rorou could go. Bendlin and Dridden watched as the younger Chimera was buried alive.

"So ... this is how we die? In a dark hole of a cursed tower, hoping the end comes before he does," Bendlin said with something approaching dark humor.

Dridden looked at him, furious. "I have *never* understood why you all are so eager to die." Bendlin recoiled as if slapped. "This is why I hold you all in such contempt."

He shouldered his way past the smaller man. The nine steps it took him to stand before Kasik the Violator were excruciating, each one requiring more courage than the last.

"Been a while since I had a redhead," Kasik rumbled. His voice was deep and booming, even muffled by the mask. He sounded other-worldly, like something from the great below.

"I am Dridden, son of Grond, prince of the Whitelands. It was my father who put you here. Do you remember?"

Kasik seemed to reflect, though it was impossible to know for sure with his face completely obscured. "I remember. How is the old man? How is the queen?" Kasik taunted.

Twelve years ago, Kasik grew bored with skulking around the outskirts and decided to take his power to the capital to challenge the throne.

"My mother walks with her kin beyond," Dridden said, more than a bit of pain in his words.

"I did do a number on her," Kasik said with a self-satisfied chuckle. "Then you are a gift; I get mama *and* baby."

Dridden could feel the man licking his lips behind that sickening mask. "Do you remember what I said to you? That day in the throne room?" Dridden choked out, water rimming his angry eyes.

He didn't think about things that upset him. Unwanted thoughts got shoved down into the pit of his mind, burned as fuel for the never-ending wars across the Whitelands. Talking about his mother was torture. It would've been easier for him to saw his own arm off.

"No, I don't remember. But I remember your ma; she made delicious 'ouch' faces."

Kasik was enjoying tearing this prince apart. Nothing brought him much pleasure but of the few things that did, breaking strong men was at the top of his list.

"I told you, when you die, my face will be the last thing you see."

"Big talk, little man. Better than you have tried."

"I know. I watched them fall. Dead at your disgusting simple-minded feet. But I figured you out. I know what they didn't. I know how to kill you."

"Rah, rah, rah. This is getting old and my little friend is waking up," Kasik said, rubbing his massive crotch.

"Are you gonna kill me, Kasik the Violator? Like all the men and women and children you killed without mercy, you sick sack of shit?"

"Eventually."

Dridden raised his voice "You hear that?! He's gonna kill me! I'll be dead!"

A blur flew past. A breeze followed that nearly took the prince off his feet. After came a boom that echoed and reverberated off the stone. He set his feet and looked up. Kasik was on his ass in the pile of ceiling rubble. Shefa stood over him, the specter of death. Piercing jade light blazing from his eyes cast the world in a heinous light.

Dridden sagged with relief. He knew the king from the south would spend his own life, but he'd promised to keep Dridden safe and he didn't believe any force could make that man a liar.

Kasik was confused. He didn't know what happened. He couldn't remember the last time something had knocked him down. He shook off the shock, started to climb to his feet. Shefa grabbed the man by the ankle and swung him through the nearest wall. Kasik went through stone like paper and landed on the other side, tumbling in a landslide.

The man roared and sprang to his feet. He wasn't hurt. He was insulted. He grabbed a fistful of bricks and launched it at Shefa. He dodged easily and the missiles hit the wall with such force they exploded on impact.

Dridden looked at Shefa; he was favoring his left leg. Kasik's magic turned any force against him back on his attacker, so Shefa just threw himself through a solid stone wall. And he was still standing!

Shefa grabbed the man's statue with one hand and shoved it across the floor to him. The room they stood in was wide open, probably an armory before it was picked clean by the inmates. There was just enough room to die running.

Kasik wrapped his meaty paw around the rear leg of the horse and charged, dragging the thing behind him, throwing golden sparks in the grey gloom. Shefa rushed out to meet him. The statue came down with a crash that shook the floor, and the ceiling rained dust. Shefa dodged by inches, staying close enough to strike back.

He threw all his weight and momentum behind an overhand left hook. His gauntlet slammed into the man's ribs with a thunderous retort. Kasik didn't feel the blow but he was driven back a step. Shefa's ring flared.

Kasik went into a rage, slamming a ton of cast bronze, again and again, swatting at Shefa like a bug, trying to smash him into the stone. Shefa dodged and rolled, left then right, before jumping back out of range.

"You can't dance forever, little man," Kasik taunted.

"Dragon."

Shefa broke right, circling around the large man. He looped him once, twice, three times.

"What are you doing?"

"Buying time," Shefa said, continuing his jog.

Kasik stopped then, remembering that this intruder didn't come alone. Where were the other three? Shefa struck him, hard, that gauntleted hand plowing into the man's hip with devastating force. Had he been a bull, it would have shattered its pelvis. Kasik slid sideways, cutting a furrow in the scattered rubble. Again, the blow didn't hurt, but it was seriously pissing him off.

He threw his weapon at Shefa, who skidded to a stop to avoid being sideswiped. Kasik charged behind the missile, slammed into him while he was distracted, driving him hard into the wall and through to the hallway beyond. They landed in a heap. Broken stone and jagged rocks dug painfully into Shefa's side and legs. Dust choked the air. Every breath Shefa took in, he coughed back out. Kasik laid a giant hand on Shefa's chest, reaching up for his throat.

"I'm gonna break your legs," he said, climbing atop the Chimera. "Then I'm gonna break your arms," as he started to squeeze. "Then I'm gonna fuck your guts out."

Kasik climbed to his feet, bring Shefa up with him by the neck. He rubbed Shefa's pained face against his stained putrid mask, laughing as he struggled against it. Bulging red veins spread from the corners of Shefa's eyes to his pupils. His face started to purple as his arms and legs went limp. Shefa gurgled something. Kasik held him out at arm's length and squeezed harder. Shefa gurgled again.

"Are you trying to talk to me?" Shefa nodded what little he could. "Why, what you got to say to me that I would wanna hear? Some clever last words? Not interested, pretty sure I heard'em all by now anyway."

And he continued squeezing.

Shefa was dying. He knew the sensation well. The dust was collecting in his eyes. Blinking did nothing for it. He could feel a cloud caking in his nostrils. He couldn't breathe, no air out, no air in. His lungs burned. A migraine exploded in the back of his head like a slow turning drill. Veins in his eyes were popping, his vision fading to black. The muscles in his neck were being crushed against his spine and he couldn't feel anything below the chest.

Shefa created a telepathic link with Kasik.

"I was trying to tell you—" The man panicked as the strange voice spoke in his thoughts. *"Time's up."*

Purble energy flared and formed a perfect bubble around Kasik's head. He dropped Shefa immediately, hands going to the new threat. Shefa hit the ground too hurt to do anything but wheeze. Kasik panicked, wading left and right, back and forth as he breathed all the air trapped in the dome.

Kasik focused. He found Rorou standing down the hall, clothes tattered from climbing out of the debris, arms out, straining. Clearly, he was the one responsible. Kasik grabbed a pile of wreckage and whipped it at him. Rorou dodged and it cost him his focus. Kasik reared back and slammed his head on the ground with a silent roar, shattering the construct to stardust.

The killer rolled on his back, starving for air, heaving in great lung-fulls seemingly immune to the swirling cloud of dust. He opened his eyes when Shefa laid a hand on his chest. With a jerk, Shefa ripped off the chain the man wore as a belt. Kasik shoved him off.

Shefa *KINRUSHED*, shooting forward in a flash, a hard left hand to the chest knocked the large man back against the wall. Shefa watched his ring flare violently. Kasik lunged forward, trying to get his hands around Shefa's neck again. Shefa dodged the clumsy attack and ripped off the man's garment.

Kasik spun around in a defensive crouch. He stood naked and hulking; Shefa could hear his heart pounding from there. The man wasn't used to exercise.

"Trying to get a look at the goods, huh?"

Shefa's voice was bruised and raspy. "Prince..."

Dridden stepped into the hall. Kasik looked at him, confused. Dridden mimed taking off a mask. He could see the man's shock from there. Purble light coalesced around Kasik's wrists and ankles. Another flash bonded the two sets of shackles together. Shefa kicked the man in the back of the knee and pulled him down on his back, the magic of the mask taking him down too.

Shefa jumped on his chest and rained down punches. Hard punches. Fast punches. Each one would've killed a normal man. Booming impacts were too close together to echo. Shefa punched him thirty-seven times in three seconds. His *KINSTONE* ring was blinding! Squatting on the man's chest, Shefa tugged at his mask.

A solid plate of iron *bolted* to the man's head so it could never be removed, so he could never be caught off guard ... Shefa pulled. Kasik screamed. Shefa pulled. Kasik struggled. Shefa pulled and pulled until he could no longer hear Kasik over his own efforts and with a sound like pouring hot stew over cold stones, he tore the mask off and half the man's face with it.

Shefa's *KINSTONE* ring would absorb incoming damage but pressure was completely different. As Shefa pulled at that mask, none of his magic could help him. Not his armor. Not his *KINSTONES*. He felt every ounce of what Kasik went through.

Together they raged! Screaming and flopping around the ruined hallway, crying in excruciating pain. Shefa could feel the holes in his skull, jagged things that hurt too deep to describe. Kasik was bleeding like a spigot, and while Shefa felt the pain, his hands didn't come away wet.

Dridden dragged Shefa away and toward his friend. He watched Kasik wail in what looked liked unbelievable agony. Dridden walked over and stomped down on the wailing man's back. With no particular urgency, he cut the tendons at the back of his knees. Then he cut both Achilles' tendons. The man muttered unintelligibly, sputum flowing freely from his nose. Long ropes of dust-caked slobber trailed to the floor.

"Just kill me. Just kill me," the man begged over and over again.

Dridden got down and looked the man in the eye. "That ... is pain. You probably forgot what it feels like hiding behind that mask, but you remember now, don't you?"

"Please, I'm sorry. Just kill me." He whined like a frightened child.

"This is the feeling you have passed around to everyone, everywhere you went. You love this, remember? The way they scream, the faces they make..."

"Fuck you! I hate you! Y-y-your ma, the queen? Ha! I fucked her, I fucked her good! In your pa's chair! R-r-right in the throne room! Couldn't nobody do nothing to stop me. You should've been there. You should've seen it. Seen her cry, and bleed ... seen her ... seen her. She felt it, you know? When I filled her with my seed, she could feel it. I saw it, in her face ... she knew it..."

"I have been angry my life because of you. Felt weak. Powerless.

My father became as cold the peaks after you shamed him. All that hate and regret landed right on my shoulders. You can't hurt me anymore."

Dridden stood up. He didn't wipe the tears cutting clean streaks down his dirty face. He let them be. They represented all the dark in him that he couldn't get out any other way. Those tears were poison. It felt good to unburden himself. To unshackle himself from this monster. To finally let go.

"You can say whatever you like. Because it won't change a thing. I'm gonna take you home, to my father so he can see what you are, what you really are. Nothing. Then I'm going to take you to every city, village, hamlet, and hut in the Whitelands. You will be whipped and spit on, humiliated and mocked. Entire towns will line up to piss on your head. I'll offer a reward for the most vile. And through it all, I will keep you alive. That's how *I* fuck, you worthless piece of shit."

"My prince ... we should go."

"You go ahead, *Lakuu*. I'm gonna stay for a while."

Bendlin walked away from the young man, knowing that as dark as this was, he needed it. To exorcise his demons, to cleanse the wound with fire. When he got to the Chimera, he looked back at the boy who used to bounce on his knee, seeing not only that child, but the man he'd become and the man he still had the potential to be.

"He called you *Lakuu?*" Rorou asked.

"It means uncle."

The prospect of death brings a clarity nothing else can.

Rorou helped Shefa to the next floor. He hadn't seen him so ... reduced, since they were small children. As they left the stairs and entered into the vestibule, Shefa collapsed. On his hands and knees, he wept. Not audibly, just a pitiful bobbing of the shoulders and hard sniffles as his nose ran freely.

As tears, hot in the frozen room, steamed on the stone only to freeze a moment later, the underdeveloped boy he still was became openly visible. He wasn't physically wounded, but the phantom pain from tearing off his own face still lingered. Bendlin couldn't watch and turned away.

For minutes, the most powerful boy either of them had ever seen was completely vulnerable. Rorou watched his king, his clanmate, his friend, suffer. Powerless, he stood by in silence, choking down his own tears at the sight. There was no place, no time in those long brutal moments; only a misery that nothing but time could wash away.

After half an hour, Shefa finally blew out a long emptying breath and blew his nose. Sitting back on his heels, he closed his eyes; hands laid neatly on his thighs, and composed himself.

"That *REALLY* hurt," he said with a compromised chuckle.

The group attempted to humor him. He sprung to his feet, flexing a few times to stretch out his knees and back, and for the first time, the group noticed the room.

Whatever this place was before the dwarves left, *this* was the room meant to impress. The floor was built of amethyst, each tile smaller than a man's hand, cut into complex geometric shapes seamlessly spliced together that appeared to be red Dwarves facing left and yellow hammers facing right.

The room would take thirty paces to cross from east to west, twice that north to south. A beautiful stone that was neither marble nor granite but some amazing impossible offspring of both arched across the room to support the ceiling, eliminating the need for columns which would've obscured the breathtaking view.

No drapes or paintings on the walls, but images of noble dwarves were cut into reliefs set into the wall, each made up of hundreds of thousands of grains of painted sand. Each relief stood taller than any two of them in the room; a total of twelve monuments covered the walls. Etched into the stone between them was old Dwarven script, presumably identifying those immortalized there.

Several of the precious stones had been chipped out from the floor.

Shefa guessed it was how the bandits financed their weapons and armor.

"This must be the most beautiful thing in the entire world," Bendlin whispered in breathless wonder.

Shefa nodded. It was indeed beautiful, but he had seen things no other mortal had or likely ever would. He let the man have his moment. Rorou ran tentative fingers over the gems, marveling at the craftsmanship. Shefa wandered to the far end of the room, noting how clean it was; no dust or garbage, not even cobwebs. Perfectly preserved somehow. A grand door exited the room but before it and to the right, a small alcove, easily missed, grabbed his eye. He slipped inside.

Food. Pounds of food. Tons of food. An entire garden of mushrooms, vegetables, berry and fruit trees. The room could not be big enough to contain what it held, yet it did. Fruit hung fat and juicy on timeless trees; apples, plums, oranges, and apricots. The room was lit in pure sunlight though there were no windows, no skylight.

He plucked a plum from a tree, feeling it in his fingers. It was as perfect a specimen as he had ever seen. Just before he bit into it he noted movement. His eyes snapped to. Already a new bud was replacing what he had taken.

Marvelous, he thought.

Then he gorged himself heavy.

The group filled their bellies with a glee not usually found in hostile territory, almost forgetting the danger that completely surrounded them. Through the grand doors at the back of the greeting room, they entered a dilapidated husk of a room that seemed intentionally antithetical to the one before.

The boards of wooden plank flooring were bowed and splintered. Chandeliers hung empty and caked in dust. Twelve lamps fixed to the walls seemed to be the only things in working order. They cast the room in a tone of somber sunset. Every hair on Rorou's body stood on end.

"Caution," he whispered.

The Northman adjusted his grip on his Axis.

"You have cost me much," a husky voice said. It was feminine, but not necessarily female. "What do you want?"

"Rest," Rorou blurted.

Silence.

"I am Shefa DragonPaw, lord of Fuumashon, future king of all the world. I have come to put an end to the bandits terrorizing this region."

Silence.

"You are the dragon boy from my dreams," the voice said. Not a question.

Shefa looked at Rorou. Rorou shrugged then smirked. "Don't be so impressed with yourself, Shefa; women dream of me as well," Rorou charmed.

"Are you lord here?" Shefa asked

"Here? Is there such a place where I am not?"

"I know at least one," Shefa said. "It is not a necessity that you die. An end to the raids is what I seek so that the rightful monarch can rule in peace."

"The *rightful* monarch? This land did not always belong to men. Men came with sword and ax and took this land. How is what I'm doing any different?"

Rorou turned to Shefa. "She's got a point."

"Roo," which meant shut up, was all he said.

"This land belongs to my people, bought and paid for with mountains of bodies and oceans of blood. You don't belong here!" Bendlin said.

Silence.

"I would prefer if you'd show yourself."

"All who have seen me feel the same," the voice said with a self-satisfied chuckle.

Rorou smirked again. "I am loving her confidence."

"Roo." Shefa sighed. "Come out."

The world before him fluttered down like a curtain cut free of its strings, revealing a throne, a simple affair of wood and gold and a most unexpected occupant upon it. She was tall, beautiful, powerful. She was Chimera.

"Beautiful," Bendlin said.

"Beautiful things are the most dangerous," Rorou warned.

"Dangerous things are the most beautiful," Shefa replied.

MIRROR

"INSIDE AND OUT"

She was beautiful in a way that only Kaharh had ever been to him. She looked like to kiss her was to die, screaming. His lips tingled hungrily at the thought.

"Who are you?"

"You killed who-knows-how-many to get here, bathed in how much blood? And *that's* your first question?"

"Yes."

They said nothing for long, uncomfortable minutes. Blink. Breathe. Nothing else. The gauntlet was affecting him. His animal nature was suppressing his ability to think. She was beautiful—well, not *just* beautiful—she looked like the odd shaped piece of him that was missing.

Shefa started to take a step.

"Sheva."

"Sheva?"

"Yes. My name is Sheva."

"What are you?"

"Perfection," she said without flare or arrogance.

She stated a fact as simple as heat is hot. And she was. Shefa's height. A warrior's build. The same large, slanted eyes as his mother, black as ink's shadow but lit from within, littered with purple metallic flakes that whispered to him in a language only his soul understood. Covered in a rainbow of scales, hot-fire pink, fuchsia, and plum. Horns like the head of a blacksmith's hammer, too black to shine, even in the light of a thousand candles.

Draped in white gossamer so thin she might as well have been naked, her boots were made entirely of human teeth and finger bones. A medallion with a jewel the size of a saucer hung from her off-the-hip belt. Tanzanite; it changed color every couple of degrees. People standing in the same room would see completely different colors. Tanzanite was the best stone for storing kinetic energy. The elves called it Angelstone; it was perfect armor.

Shefa started to step again, ready to get this over with. As if she could feel his intention, she spoke.

"So eager. You must be a passionate and terrible lover." She smiled as though she had found the key to a treasure chest. Her lips, heart shaped, were full and inviting.

Shefa's face went blank for a fraction of a second, barely noticeable. Barely. He recovered and made no attempt to hide his emotion. He was saddened. The only person he had ever made love to sacrificed their love for Fuumashon. It hurt. It always hurt. It always would.

"I can't figure out if you're trying to save yourself, or trying to get in my head."

"Maybe I'm just inviting you to my bed," she said, blinking her eyes slowly, intently. It was a ploy, but to sell it she would, without hesitation, lay with him and likely show him things a faithful lover never could.

Shefa shrugged. "I'm not tired."

"We wouldn't sleep."

Rorou stepped forward. "Perhaps I can—"

"SILENCE!" she screamed at him.

A wailing, maddened, unhinged thing belted out at the top of her lungs. The transformation was frighteningly sudden. Her voice filled the room. The walls themselves seemed to bow away from her.

"*HE* may speak here. Not you, not your human pet. You are alive because *HE* intrigues me." She turned her attention back to Shefa, all malice gone, sex kitten returned. "Do you know what *we* are?"

"No."

"We are perfect castings from a flawed mold."

"You presume much."

She looked at him with an expression he couldn't read. There was a war going on inside her. Shefa decided he would wait to see which side won.

"I searched for you, you know?"

"No," Shefa said.

"I was told of you ... by Saber."

Shefa said nothing for a while. "Saber is dead," he said with mock confidence.

"I fixed him."

"I turned him inside out."

She smirked something sexy. "I didn't say it was easy."

Shefa was enthralled. His loins were distracting him. Nothing excited him like power, except possibly breaking something powerful. Somewhere in the back of his mind, he was aware that the gauntlet was affecting him, but it was a child's whisper in a storm. There was something between them, a connection he couldn't define or explain ... or ignore.

"Why are you terrorizing these people? You can do whatever you want, go wherever you want, take whatever you want; why waste time in this frozen asshole of a country?"

"Fuumashon is impossible to find. Whoever hid it, hid it well. After wasting years of my life, I decided you were a myth, didn't exist. This is where I was, and I just kinda stayed," she answered with a shrug.

Shefa looked at her with something halfway between sympathy and suspicion. She had likely lived a life very similar to his. Likely, he thought...

"You know what I am?" he asked.

"A puzzle, like me. No womb, no night of passion between strangers. No, you are a creation. Elf-craft, if I had to guess. Somebody somewhere plucked you from the earth, hammered and purified you, and turned you into a living weapon. Just like me," she said, adjusting herself so that her breasts swayed ever so slightly.

Shefa felt a pang of guilt for wanting to kill her. They were two sides of the same coin. Maybe in some distant corner of the world, she was a queen, saving her people from a fate the rest of the world was wholly ignorant to.

"I am Chimera. Created by the emerald mistress and her acolytes to save my homeland from a war like no other. I was born a dragon and like all dragons, I could not remain a slave. I accomplished my mission, I fulfilled my purpose, and now I'm free. This world is mine. There will be peace, there will be order. Will you have to die first?"

"Maybe."

Shefa said nothing.

"How was your childhood?" she asked.

"Over too soon," he said.

"Same. How stands your heart?"

"Empty," he said.

"Same. Did you love her?" she asked.

The question kicked Shefa's chest in. Was it a guess? How did she know there *was* a her? What was her game? Rorou cleared his throat, reminding Shefa he was in the room. Shefa couldn't believe he had forgotten. Bendlin as well. Nothing existed but the ravishing creature in front of him.

"Did you love her?" she repeated.

"With all of me."

"So, the mighty warrior, heartbroken and spurned, wanders the world searching for meaning." Her tone was light but not mocking. "There is no meaning. We are here, someday we won't be. Until then, we do what we can, suffer what we must, and take what pleasures we find. Maybe ... you are the temperance I need, and I am the challenge you seek."

"Can we kill this bitch already?" Bendlin seemed exasperated.

There was a boom, and then he was sailing backward through the air. He bounced off the wall, hit the ground and lay still, *perfectly* still. Shefa stood, mouth agape, stun-locked. Sheva stood where Bendlin was a moment before, still frozen in the punch that launched his friend across the room. Rorou looked at Bendlin, concerned. Concern turned swiftly to rage.

He twitched. Shefa moved. Sheva vanished. Rorou flew from his feet, twisting and turning in ways no humanoid body was meant to. He pulled out of his spin at the last moment and landed on his feet. His hands flew to his chest; he looked up, terrified, then collapsed in an unnatural heap.

Shefa didn't get there in time to save his friend; he got there just in time for her to grab him by the throat. It seemed like an hour later when the boom from the impact reached his ears. No one was this fast. No *thing* was this fast.

"What. Are. You?" Shefa ground out.

Sheva's lethal visage relaxed. "I am ... bored."

She let him go. He wanted to kill her, to reach inside her and pull out her guts. He didn't. He couldn't, and he didn't understand why.

"They live," she said placidly. "Killing them would hardly put me in your good graces."

She wanted something from him, he realized.

"Why do you care about my graces?"

She didn't speak for many long moments. "How long do you think we will live? A hundred years? A thousand years?"

"How old are you?" Shefa asked

"I never bothered to count. I have watched mountains become rivers and those rivers run dry."

"You're ... lonely."

"Desperately. Do you know what it is to know days, years, centuries; and to know they mean nothing? Love will fade, lovers will die and you will remain. Smaller. Colder."

She turned away, folding her arms over her chest. A breeze that he couldn't feel waved her dressing somberly.

"I knew love. It died. I found purpose beyond my creation. Why can't you?" he whispered, taking a tiny step toward her.

"I don't crave purpose. I crave passion. I want to love and be loved, to notice the sunset again. To find more than momentary pleasure atop some grunting fool who will think me his because we swapped fluids. I want to be alive again!" There was fire in her words.

Shefa moved forward, reaching. Was she? Could they be? She spun to him. His hand touched her cheek; her scales flared beneath his touch, as if dragons could blush. She nuzzled her face into his hand as they closed in on each other.

She whispered his name lovingly, "Shefa?"

"Yes?" he whispered back, hungrily.

"How have you lived this long, being this stupid?"

She punched him in the gut, a blow that lifted him off his feet. As he came to the height of his climb, she hammered him back down to the floor hard enough to bounce, then kicked his bouncing body across the room. Shefa curled into a ball, protecting his injured ribs. He could feel the cracks in the bones with every shallow breath. Through his pain, he could hear the *click-clack* of her tooth-and-bone boots as she approached.

He struggled to get back to his feet but just uncurling sent a firestorm up his side.

"I had hoped you would be more," she said, taking his grimacing face in her hands. "But don't worry, brave warrior. King of all Fuumashon," she said with a chuckle. "You will have purpose. You will serve me."

She kissed him deep on his trembling lips. His pain melted away. The floor fell out from beneath him and the walls went up in a puff of smoke. All white.

His vision returned sometime later; he found himself on a beach, waves lapping the shore, licking his naked toes. He was in Fuumashon. It didn't matter that he had never seen *this* place before. The land of his birth *felt* like home in a way no words could ever define. He wore no shirt and short pants.

The weather was in that perfect window where the world was summer in the morning yet autumn by sunset. Golden sand stretched left and right to the Crown Mountains that ringed the continent, snow-capped year-round because of their great height.

A giggling too pure to be real turned his head back to the sea. Sheva, wearing a smile so ... innocent, ascended from the waves. It made his pulse quicken just to see her. She wore just enough to cover her femininity, wet white fabric clinging to her shapely muscular form. As she rose out of the waves, his breath caught in his throat.

She carried two children, one in each arm, exuding an infectious glee that brought moisture to his eyes. He could see in their faces, in their spirit, these were his children. His and hers.

A lifetime exploded in his head. A thousand years of memories with his loving wife, ever by his side. He remembered the tower in AlinGuard where they met, how she convinced him to give her a chance to prove she could be more than her creators intended. He remembered the weeks they spent alone in that magical place, eating fruit from a tree that never went barren as she showed him all the wonders of the place she called home.

"This is my favorite room," she said

"It's beautiful," Shefa replied.

She looked at him curiously. "Beautiful? Is that all?" Now it was his turn to look puzzled. "These stones, do you know what they are?" she asked, referring to the mosaic work of jewels that covered the room. "These thousands of pieces of polished glass are not beautiful. The dwarves didn't haul them up here for vanity, though the faces on the wall might make you doubt that."

Shefa noted again the images of great dwarves, long turned to dust by now, finally realizing that while the room was covered in jewels, *they* were made from sand tables. He looked again, truly looking this time at the room he was standing in.

"Do you see it?" she asked hopefully

"There is something there, but I can't place it. Like a name whispered in a dream..."

"This..." she said indicating the entire room "...is one stone. You would call it a Chimera stone. That's why the pieces fit so perfectly together. They were once a single great jewel. The same as the one that created you."

Warning bells rang powerfully in his head then.

"With this, you could create an army," he said.

She moved closer to him, pressing her breasts against his chest, her forehead to his, peering deep into his multicolored eyes. "Not an army, a family."

His mind swirled from that memory, leaping a hundred years through time. He landed on this very beach, but the sand was a worrying shade of orange. The waves, once so blue, polluted by more blood than the fields to the south, now appeared a sickly brown, only showing red when the sun pierced the waves as they broke.

Chimera lay broken around him, a fleet of fleets blanketing the horizon, ships large enough to carry an army each. Ten thousand were already sunken, their crews face down in the surf. A finger touched his, climbing across his palm, seeking, taking his hand.

It was her. His loving wife. Broken and bleeding and standing by his side. Her hard eyes and pleading smiled filled him with hope, the fuel he would burn to save his homeland. She was his rock, his salvation, his life source.

A wall of pink clouds swept him away, dropping him in Fuumindall's Horn. The Council Chamber was filled with his friends. Gala, Mim, Garrison, even Patience was there. He remembered that feeling when his clanmates embraced his lady love, their faces beaming with pride, joy radiating from them in waves. So pleased that he had finally found someone to share the years and hopefully centuries with, they took her as one of their own immediately.

He loved the way she looked in his colors, draped in blue and white, covered in Cyan colored jewels, his nation's flag emblazoned on the hem of her every garment. He could live in that moment forever.

He remembered the thousands of hours spent in his mother's library, searching for the spell that brought them into being. Countless tomes and scrolls combed through with obsessive scrutiny. Kaharh, the former love of his life, gave them not only the means to achieve their goal, but her blessing, which meant more to him than any collection of words could express.

The war won, Fuumashon was the center of commerce for the known world. It was time to start a family. He remembered that first attempt. So much pain. They created life but it wasn't stable. A brief flash of pain and madness before returning to the ether, for all their efforts they only had sorrow to show for it.

The second attempt was better but not the offspring they had dreamed of. Then came Alvera, Shefa's firstborn. A son to inherit the world and carry on his name. Shefa didn't remember this time as a moment or an event; it wasn't a physical thing that a label hung easily on. It was the feeling he had when Heaven's light kissed him, only it didn't fade. There was nothing left for him in this world but to hold his wife and watch their son grow. This was fulfillment.

His daughter, Sitara, was a surprise. Crafted in secret as a gift for him, he welcomed her with all his heart. Life was perfect. Swirls of blue and gold embraced him, piercing him, filling his soul with an ecstasy his flesh could never know as unseen currents carried him down the river of dreams.

He landed on a throne, his throne, tall and golden, trimmed in platinum and pearl. Every surface bore his mother's face; beneath, the symbol of his house and his family. His wife stood before him and all his royal court, her dragon scale armor filthy with the blood of her enemies. Her handmaidens unfurled a map that detailed the whole world, a thing too large for any room but that one. Sheva touched an area of the map which turned Cyan blue under her finger and the room exploded in celebration.

"I claim this land in your name and your honor, my lord, my king, my Shefa," she said and kneeled before her husband.

As the room bowed before his glory and her magnificence, she flashed him a look that he knew well, but not often as the campaign kept her away weeks at a time. The slivers of purple in her dark globular eyes lit a fire in him that they would spend the next week bathing in.

Year after year, while his children grew, the world shrank. Conquest after conquest, expansion to the west, the north; they were perpetually at war, spreading his glory to every corner of the earth and his devoted wife always there, leading the charge.

He remembered his son marching off to war, his wife promising to return him an equal to his sire. He remembered Alvera's platinum hair and broad shoulders. He had his mother's horns, but his scales favored his father, deep emerald, so green as to appear black in certain light. He could still feel the pride of that day, and his heart was happy.

Years became decades, and every day his kingdom grew, every day his name reached new ears, everyday more souls kneeled before his flag. Soon there was nothing but Cyan on that map. There was no place that did not know the name Shefa, Fuumashon, or the face of his blade: Sheva, the destroyer of worlds.

He opened his eyes. Sheva still held his face, cupped delicately in her strong hands. He was back in the frozen north, in a stolen tower, and he could still feel the thousands upon thousands of kisses she had laid on his lips over their long, happy life together. The pain in his body was gone. His friend and his charge lay in a heap across the room, but he couldn't bring himself to care.

"My lord, my king, my Shefa ... make me your wife and I will make you king of all the world, just as you desire," she whispered, painfully seductive.

Her voice cut through him without resistance, a sword made of love, sharpened by hate. Her words, a dagger crafted from a halo and just as beautiful to behold.

"Lift me," he said. She pulled him to his feet, her love and admiration for him permanently carved into her face, deep as bone. Shefa took three steps back. "You had my heart. You had my life, vile betrayer, but for one thing."

"Husband?" She was so worried then.

"I wanted what you offered. So ... completely. I would've followed you, let you lead me around by the nose for a thousand years. Even knowing what you are."

"What I am is yours, my love. Wholly and completely. Devoted above all others."

"Silence," he whispered. His eyes turned down to the floor, unable to look at her, shame for his desperation weighing his head down, slumping his shoulders. "You are a monster."

"We are both monsters, that's why we belong together, Sheath. Don't you see?"

"Silence," he whispered again. She pressed her lips obediently together. "I am a weapon. I was created to destroy. The difference is I never needed a leash. I don't crave the blood. I don't kill to feel alive. My power does not come from dominating others."

Sheva started moving forward, reaching a contrite hand to his face. "Come, my love. I will take your troubles away. Remember my bed? Remember the bliss we always found there?"

And he did. He could still feel her nails peeling his flesh apart as he ripped her from the inside. Her teeth sinking into his neck, his hands pinning her down as she mock struggled to get away. The smell of their love, thick in the air. The sparkling iridescent cloud their lust made. His bedchamber a ruin in the aftermath of their coupling. He could still feel it.

What was he thinking? Was he going to throw away one thousand years over this? Some petty fight over ... what were they fighting over again? He couldn't even remember; that's how trivial it was. He looked then at his wife. A pulse ran through him, a millennium of happiness reborn within his chest. He felt the tears coming. Her hand touched his face and he knew it was all real, true as the heat of the sun.

"Take me," she cooed as she nibbled his ear.

"Kaharh," he huskily whispered back.

Sheva recoiled as if struck. "She is beautiful. Dangerous. The only thing I truly fear. What she is *not* is gracious or forgiving. If not for her giving us her blessing, you would have won."

Her face went hard, the loving mask gone in a blink. She still held his face. He could feel her influence, a sickly-sweet scent in his nose, tea too sweet to drink. His skin slithered away from her touch.

"I always win." She moved in to kiss him again. He whispered into her mouth, the kiss mumbling the words. "What was that, my love?" she asked with supreme confidence. She had played this game many times and she always found the key to victory.

"I said, speak again and I will rip you inside out."

It took her a moment to process the unexpected words. Shefa casually placed his hand on her chest, his heart heavy, his eyes leaking scalding salt water. His wife and partner of more than a lifetime was there for the taking, if only he would embrace her—instead, he pushed her back to arm's length ... with his left hand.

"I know who I want to be, but that is not who I am. I know who I am. I am Shefa DragonPaw, firstborn of the emerald mistress, Emma-fuumindall, lord of all Fuumashon, future king of all the world. I have seen the realm of light. I have shattered its champion. I am the sword unsheathed. You are my next victim."

Sheva hadn't moved a muscle but now she seemed anxious, bubbling with an energy she had no home for. "I am Sheva, first of my name, first and last of my kind. I am the realized dream of a madman who acquired so much wealth, his fear of losing it squeezed out every-thing else. I am the Host of Dragon. Red, blue, white, and amethyst. I am a bandit, a thief, a killer, and a whore. I have burned towns to the ground. I have broken babies in half while their mothers watched. I have hunted and killed every creature on this planet. And I enjoyed it all."

She stood directly in front of him. There was no fear. He knew she wanted to get him, to break him, to own him. She was just like him. He watched her look at him, not his eyes; she was inspecting him. He was a prize to her, bought and paid for and now she was evaluating her purchase. He couldn't help but do the same. The way she moved, shifting hips, sparkling savage eyes, filled with a passion bordering on rage; she was lust made flesh.

Shefa whispered breathlessly, "Ready?"

She whispered back, "Yes."

He nodded. She smiled. Twitch.

He punched at her face. If the blow landed, it would have caved in her skull. She dodged the exact degree necessary to avoid the blow while returning with a punch of her own. He twisted in place, letting the punch slip by, the miss creating a sonic boom. He threw a right hook at her head. She ducked, right into his rising knee. Only after impact did she realize the punch was a feint.

The knee stood her back up. Shefa grabbed her by the throat, snatched her off her feet and choke slammed her head first into the ground. When his hand slammed into the ground, she wasn't in it. Confused, he looked up just in time to see her boot of teeth and bones slam into his side and all the pain from before came back in a swal-lowing rush.

"Yes, fight back. Make me work for it. What dragon doesn't want to hunt its prey?" Sheva hissed, deep into her madness.

Shefa rolled onto his knees, holding his side, casting the meager healing spells he knew, hoping she would keep talking until he could think again.

"Before you die, you will know it. Know ... that you could have done nothing to stop it." She smirked.

"Stalling? How ... human," he teased.

She was a blur, magenta streaks across his vision, and then the world spun in conflicting circles before a volcano of agony erupted in his back. He didn't even know what she had done to him. Shefa was a weapon, designed and crafted. There was no place for empathy in a hate machine.

His time with the elves, with the humans, had created a schism, dueling personalities within the same flesh. His inner dragon fought to break free, to turn the Sheath into the Sword, a thing he spent most his life trying to tame. Here, with death inescapable, the dragon refused to go quietly into the dark. The boy simply stopped fighting.

"Shall we continue this later? After you've had a rest, small meal perhaps?" she said, mocking his struggle, unaware of the war he was fighting on her behalf.

Shefa found his feet. "The boy sends you his regards."

She flinched involuntarily at the strange comment. "Does he now?"

"Fear not; you will have a moment to say goodbyes."

The Sword charged. Sheva timed his movements, anticipating the moment he would arrive in range then beat him to the spot. She flew like a diving hawk, head first into his surprised face. The impact reversed his forward momentum, the boom swept dust across the floor like a summer gale. The Sword took the blow in stride, catching her ankle before she could sail past. Twisting in midair, he whipped her into the ground like a heavy chain, teeth exploding out of her mouth on impact.

She was stunned. Not at the pain, she had known worse, but the move itself was impossible! She stared at her shattered teeth on the dirt covered floor, speechless. Splinters filled the roof of her mouth, inciting a coughing fit as her body fought to dislodge them. He punted her between the legs, flipping her head over heel to land awkwardly on her shoulder. Red stained her dress.

She buried the pain, rolled with the landing and came back at him in a rush. The Sword stepped forward, slamming into her before she could execute her attack. He bounced her back but she clawed into the ground, straightened her leg and skidded to a stop before she was carried out of attack range.

They stood face to face, alphas asserting their dominance. They threw punches without blocks or parries. Thirty, fifty, a hundred in a row. Limbs a blur of motion, the crystalline clacks of impact playing out like a duel between drummers.

Scales cracked. Bones buckled. Neither of them gave any ground. There was no sense in this fight, no reason. Two animals willing to die to kill their enemy. Sheva raised her foot. The Sword dodged in anticipation, only she didn't kick. She brought her foot down like thunder.

A cone of devastating kinetic energy exploded beneath him, launching him into the ceiling. He hit the stone hard enough to rattle the braziers mounted on the wall. As he fell, he noted the blade in her hand.

Seemingly from nowhere, she produced a blade like he had never seen; triangular, made of a silvery-white metal mounted on a two-handed staff. It looked like an arrowhead stretched two feet too far. She meant to skewer him as he dropped. Pitiful move. The Sword drew his tool, crafting it into a scimitar in his plummet and met her blade to blade. His feet hit the ground; she strengthened her stance and the battle began anew.

Steel flashed too bright to stand, creating a blinding strobing effect. When they couldn't see they turned to their other senses, relying on sound and smells, the shifting weight on the floor to track each other and they never missed a beat. The scream of metal on metal was a constant warbling wail that grated on nerves and teeth.

Neither gave ground. Neither ever thought to. Sweat ran down his brow, stinging his eyes, he fought on. Blood pooled in her mouth from her broken teeth; she swallowed and fought on. Sheva didn't notice the strikes that slipped through her guard, turned away by her scales.

Chips and flakes of pink glinted in the muted light, dust motes sailing through afternoon sunbeams.

The Sword wasn't aware of the drops of blood, flash-boiled to steam from the heat of her blade, surrounding him like the morning fog in the mountains of his homeland. They were grunting with each swing, huffing with each block, each parry, muscles trembling spastically from the violent vibrations of each impact. Two masters of equal skill, equal resolve, pushing themselves and each other their limits then beyond. Neither would quit. Neither would give. Only boldness, the willingness to sacrifice for victory would tip the scales.

Sheva released her blade, the Sword's strike swatted it across the room where it stuck fast in the far wall, handle first, quivering as though in an earthquake. The lack of resistance made him overbalance. She used that moment to duck the return blow, inhale deeply and release a gale of biting blue fire in his face.

The pain was instantaneous. It felt as though his eyes were melting out of his skull. Any sane creature would have retreated, if only tactically, while its eyes, nose, and throat roasted. The Sword was not a sane creature. The Sword charged. He slammed into her, a falling star.

Still breathing blue flame, she couldn't catch her breath, his shoulder driving what little air she had left out in a mad rush. They hit the far wall, a chorus of screams like cracking glass let him know the scales on her back were ruined. The wall bucked, struggling to stay standing as he ground her through it and into the hall beyond.

They landed in a heap of bricks and dust, a cloud of stone covered them. They fought on, rolling over jagged edges, coughing and wheezing even as they fought to gain the upper hand in the scramble. She kicked him off of her. He took the blow, sailing away from his prey, using the opportunity to summon his most powerful spell, *EXPLODET!*

Raw cosmic energy drawn from the nether came to him. Without shaping or defining it, he released it in a storm. Pure energy that could be shaped into light or heat, thunder or health, in its raw form, was the most destructive force in nature.

The far wall of the showing room exploded, sound waves crushing the organs inside him. Thousand-year-old stone was obliterated; the dust that remained flew from the tower in a torrent, cutting a dark grey scar across the snow-white sky.

The foundation of the tower shifted, throwing off the delicate balance the builders achieved all those centuries ago. Stone groaned as the structure threatened to topple. Rorou and Bendlin, limp and unconscious, were thrown haphazardly into walls and each other from the blowback created by the overpressure.

Sheva lay face down, struggling to rise. Half her scales were stripped from her flesh. Bright pink blood ran in a thousand rivulets from her broken skin. The Sword looked at her without pity. With a thought, he lifted from the ground, hovering toward his prey. A twinge in the back of his mind shook his focus.

He knew this feeling, too well. There was a time when he would have fought it, but he had seen too much to think this was a fight that could be won. He would bide his time and return when the boy was more in touch with his true self. The dragon bowed out gracefully, holding his anger for the next time.

Shefa came back with a scream. Sweat-covered and panting, his first thought was his friends. He ran back to the hole in the wall, leaped across the ruined hall, charging into Sheva's chamber panicked. He found Rorou and Bendlin in a corner beneath a pile of dust and debris.

He clapped his hands mightily, blowing the filth away, checking them for breathing. He sagged with relief when he found a pulse. Mindless of everything else in existence, he dedicated his whole being to healing, to channeling a river of restoring energy to his clanmates.

After time indeterminate, Rorou coughed himself awake. Shefa moved his hand, now placing both of them on Bendlin, hoping he could bring the man back before he himself passed out. Far away he heard his name. He ignored it, he couldn't be distracted now. Then he heard it again and again, his name, screamed at him, beggingly.

I know that voice, he thought.

In a flash he came back, sprawled on the ground, Rorou and Bendlin shaking him more than a little rudely. He didn't remember falling. He was tired, deep down bone-weary exhausted. He could feel the magic of his boots funneling energy to him but he had pushed himself beyond even their power.

"Get them out," Shefa croaked.

"Come, I'll carry you."

"No, Roo. I made a promise. Get them and get out. I'm right behind you."

Rorou looked at him suspiciously. "Off to collect a trophy?"

"Off to make sure that bitch is dead."

Rorou nodded sharply then helped Bendlin traverse the severely compromised stairs.

Shefa picked his way back to Sheva's body. She was breathing, raggedly. She looked like a discarded toy, broken and tossed in the trash, there in that pile rubble. Still beautiful.

"Had you just told me you could change, I would have pretended to believe you."

His words were heavy with sorrow. He knew she had put those feelings and memories in his head, but his heart didn't. A lie you believe is as real as any truth.

"There is ... st-still room ... in my ... bed," she offered. One beautiful star filled eye still promised happiness.

"But there is no room in my heart."

He looked down at his dragonscale gauntlet and nodded to himself. This had to be done. She spoke a word he didn't know and her Angelstone released its power into the floor. The stone crumbled like rotted wood. They fell in a jumble among beams large enough to crush them flat and enough stone to bury them forever.

He watched her face; there was no panic in her eyes. As though swimming through water, she threw her hands back and flew toward him. She hit him before he could react and together they sailed to the far side of the tower.

They hit hard. Launched in different directions, Shefa's mind was on his friends and if they'd managed to escape in time. He hurt. Everything hurt. Thinking how bad everything hurt *hurt*. He could feel blood pooling in his belly. He smelled blood with every aching breath.

SHEVA!

He opened his eyes, searching for her through the blood-tinged blur of his vision. She had something in her hand. Not a weapon, too small. She put it to her mouth, hand trembling, threatening to drop it. Whatever it was, she spilled half of it and cursed the gods for her luck. Shefa watched as her blood slowed and clotted. He heard the bones popping back into place.

A healing elixir, of course, he thought. "So, this is how I die?" he asked the gods, mockingly.

He could call the Sword, unleash the monster within. The same who just nearly killed his friends in its selfish thirst for blood and glory. No, he decided. He chose to live, and if need be, die without compromise. He would become the weapon he was made to be or he would not, but he would do it on his terms. That's why he walked to the top of the world. That's why he left his closest companions, his most powerful weapons. He was a dragon or a Chimera, but he couldn't be both.

"You should have left with your friends."

"I'll see them again."

She chuckled. "Many have licked my boots, but you will debase yourself so much more for me. And you will thank me for the opportunity. Get up."

Shefa cast *levitate* to make himself light enough for his fatigued muscles to lift him.

"Ready?"

"Yes."

She charged, dodging side to side, moving at the very limit of his ability to track her movements. She shouldn't have bothered. He was done fighting. She slammed into him, her fist snapping three ribs just above his hip. The blow launched him. The wall stopped him. He coughed and grunted, rolling over. He puked up a belly full of blood as he took his feet.

He was breathing heavy, blowing bloody snot bubbles with every heave. One eye wouldn't open. She smiled. She twitched. He tried to follow her but she simply vanished. When she reappeared, it was with a bloom of pain. Two ribs, deep in his armpit cracked like glass. He flipped head over feet before slamming awkwardly into the floor with a violent expulsion of breath.

She watched him struggle. He was bleeding into his lungs, drowning on land. She felt herself moistening; a moan she wasn't aware of escaped her lips. He started climbing to his feet. She thought to break him and be done with it but she wanted to see how far he would get, how tall he would stand before he kneeled.

He stopped on one knee. He held up a jewel, a twinkling pinkish stone that looked foreign, yet familiar. He twisted it back and forth slightly, catching and throwing the dull light. He had stolen a scale in her last blitz.

She laughed, a light and tinkling sound full of childish glee. It almost made Shefa laugh with her.

"Bravo. Remember this tiny victory when you clean me after my morning squat," she giggled.

Shefa made a show of placing the scale on his tongue and swallowing hard. She watched in curious anticipation.

"I hope you're not waiting for me to be wowed. You're not the first man to want *me* inside of *him* instead of the usual way around," she mocked with a rolling chuckle.

Even then the elixir was working its magic, her wounded skin hardening and healing. Soon hairs would grow, then scales, and he would have no chance, no chance at all. He will have failed. The words sounded evil.

The acid in his stomach couldn't penetrate the fireproof ceramic coating of the scale but the tentacles of the *Pform* could. Scales are unique components of anatomy. They cling to the skin like hair or warts but they are made of the same concoctions as bones. As intimate as marrow.

He dissolved her. Digested her. Then he became her. The very building blocks of what she was, rolled out before him, translated pages from a secret tome, his to pilfer at will. Everything that made her different would be absorbed and incorporated into his being.

She didn't translate light into images as he did, she could see the different wavelengths of energy that composed the elements of the world. When she looked at a man, she didn't just see his flesh: his skin tone and facial features, she saw his blood type, his heritage and his beating heart ALL in the same glance. Now he would, too. The deep red in his eyes lightened a bit at the edges to reflect the pink of her scales. But this was superfluous; this was the icing, not the cake.

She wasn't fast the way he was. She didn't use her muscles to propel her forward. Well, not *just* her muscles. She manipulated the attractive energy between all objects, pulling on those strings to move closer as well as pulling her target to her. The result was, she always arrived sooner than her victims could anticipate. Now he could as well. The *Pform* were already using the latent parts of his brain to cast the meager healing spells he knew, helping his body heal while she gloated in ignorance.

"You were used. Mistreated. Just like me. I hoped that we could share our pain, maybe heal each other. I hoped. You made me hope. And I feel dirty now. Your death will be unnecessarily brutal. I promised that if you spoke again I would rip you inside out. I keep my promises," Shefa vowed.

She grinned at the threat. "You almost lived up to the legends I'd heard ... almost. You disappoint me, dragon boy."

"If only your opinion mattered."

She roared, blue flame scorching the air. Baring her teeth, she rushed, faster than sight. Shefa could've dodged. He could've slowed her down. He probably could've blocked. Instead, he lent her his stored kinetic energy, nearly doubling her speed. They collided like planets. Chest to chest. Skull to skull. Teeth to teeth.

She hit him, tumbled up and over and kept going. He was knocked flat, having gone limp in anticipation. Broken teeth shot to the back of his throat. His nose exploded, his head screaming at him to just lie down and die. But his pride...

She bounced, skidded, righted herself and was on her feet before she lost momentum. She was confused but decided to attack before he could do, whatever he had done, again. Impossibly fast she shot at him, a translucent blur, even dragon eyes weren't that fast. But he didn't need to see; he *knew* where she would be.

Back on one knee, facing her, he thrust his left hand out with all the power left in him. Her throat slammed into his open hand like an iron rod. Her trachea snapped. Thin cracks wrapped all the way around, air seeping into the muscles of her neck, never making it to her starving lungs. Her hands flew to his forearm out of pure survival instinct.

"Poor substitute for your bed, but you like it rough, remember?"

He made a pyramid of his fingers and shoved them up between her legs, between her lips with a screeching rip of soft tissue. She released a squeal, the sound baby pigs make when the wolf's teeth sink in. He pulled her close so she could see the lack of sympathy in his eyes.

He pushed higher, up through the wall of her womb with a gush of a blood and the smell of dead fish. Her eyes widened, liquid salt forming at the corners near her busted nose. He opened his hand and closed it. A sickening tangle of wet guts squished between his fingers.

He touched his nose to hers and closed his eyes. "I could've loved you."

"I c-c-can ch-change," she squeezed out around a mouthful of blood and liquid fire tears.

"How? You're dead."

And he ripped her inside out.

ACKNOWLEDGMENTS

IF WE SERVED TOGETHER.

If we lived together.
If we sinned together.
Thank you.

SIX.

ABOUT THE AUTHOR

Crafted and trained in South Florida, Alexzander grew up in sunshine, nice weather and bad schools. Son of a professional kick boxer and a church choir director, Alexzander had a happy eclectic childhood. A student and lover of music, art and all things martial, he is a military veteran and avid anime, comic book, movie, TV and video game nerd. He received his degree in TV and Film Production as well as Communications in Frederick, Maryland where he lives with his wife and three kids. If you get the chance, you really should talk to him; awesome dude.

11662132R00092

Printed in Great Britain
by Amazon